The Seraphim Chronicles

The Seraphim Chronicles

Bill Payne

A TruthBox Publication

Cover design by Nancy Lee (Earth Communications).

ISBN - 1-928715-22-2

The Seraphim Chronicles by Bill Payne.
Copyright © 2007 Bill Payne. All rights reserved. No part of this publication may be reproduced, stored in a retrieval system, or transmitted in any form or by any means -- electronic, mechanical, photocopy, recording, or any other -- except for brief quotations in printed reviews, without the prior permission of the publisher.

Acknowledgments

A very special heartfelt thanks to Gael and Sheena Parfaite for their encouragement, friendship and support; without whom this project would not have been possible.

Deep gratitude and thanks to all my cheerleaders, encouragers and supporters and those who practically helped in the writing of this book. Thanks to Marti and Craig Seminoff, John and Elaine Moffat, Mike Lee, Colin Patterson, Matt Rawlins, Bob and Stella Teasell, Terry and Ellen Price, Eldon and Phyllis Glanville, Tedd and Jo-Anne Smith, Aaron and Ada Kelly, Janice Heijs.

Words cannot express my appreciation for all the folks, friends and family at Ridgeview Community Church in London Ontario, Canada; Dresden Community Church in Dresden Ontario, Canada and Hebron Church in Heerde, The Netherlands.

Thank you Tinie (Martina Payne) my love for never letting me give up on this book.

And thanks to Tarah (Payne) for all your help, encouragement, persistence and hard work.

Thank you Father

Dedication

This book is dedicated to four very real angels in my life:

To Mary
who now makes Heaven a better place

To Tinie
who makes my life a better life

To Tarah
my eternal little girl and the joy of my life

To my mother Marie O`Connell
who gave me life and love

The Seraphim Chronicles

****

(The Embrace of Elohim)

Prologue

All who live, who ever have and ever will, long to know the mysteries of the ages. They seek to know how their journey began and to what end their journey shall come. And on the road between the two, all and every being desires to know what purpose and value is buried deep within them.

All the affairs of heart and world are measured in life and death; in light and darkness; in good and evil, in war and peace and ultimately in truth and lies. For there is indeed a vile and violent discord in the world of man.

Above all, the heart of every sojourner asks; "Why and for what cause does this conflict rage? What ill has befallen us on our journey? What foul wind has blown us off our true course?"

Few live who know the true history of ages past. Fewer still can recall the names of those who witnessed the birth of worlds; who stood in the bright light of creation; who saw the rise of evil;

who fought against the power of the one death; and whose hands touched the prophet's dream.

Here lies, in part, the story of how all these and more came to be. It is a story of hope and love and paradise won and lost. It too is a tale of such woe and grief as to make the heart sick.

Here alone is found the story behind all stories. For these words were not scribed by ink on paper or parchment nor by hands of flesh. They were written long ago on the edge of a great crystal sea by one who saw such wonders and horrors. He was and is the seraph scribe and angel prophet who witnessed the first birth and the first death. He knew the first love and heard the first lie. He yielded a sword of light in the first war and stood helpless at the rise of darkness that covers the whole Earth even now. And still today, this ancient scribe sees and writes the dark history of all and will do so until history is no more.

Here are the true tales of all and everything.

All stories have their beginnings. This is the beginning of all stories.

****

The Embrace of Elohim

He was before all beginnings, but not a he, nor she, nor it, nor they.

He was the light and the fire. He was the music and an endless symphony. He was one but more than one. He was all and there was nothing apart from him.

He was a father. He was a mother. He was a son. He was a daughter.

He was the nameless one until the first of creation saw and spoke. And many names they gave him.

His name is "Yahweh"; the being one; the one who was and is and shall always be. He is the first and the last, the father of all creation.

His name is Adonai; the power behind all powers. He is Judge and King and Lord and heir of all.

He is "the Spirit" and the Spirit was in and beyond all. He was everywhere in everything.

He was indeed a father, true to the image, but more than a father as man knew fathers.

He was a true son but more than a son as man knew sons.

He was spirit, but more than spirit of which even angels could not fathom.

His name is Elohim; Father, Son and Spirit.

And though minds of flesh can never grasp this mystery of mysteries; one was in all, and all was in one.

And they held each other in an eternal embrace of love and joy and friendship, profound and unspeakable - Father, Son and Spirit, in the embrace of Elohim.

1

The First Beginning

There have been countless beginnings and there are more yet to come. But there was a time before all beginnings, though not a time at all. For there was no time and no space and naught but Spirit and thought and heart and love. There was light and only light, but never in the midst of darkness; no darkness and no void.

And there was music; such music.

Now there was no elsewhere; for there were no walls; no within or without; no here; no there; no now; no then.

It was a time before time - before angels and man; a time before names and naming. It was a time before the fetters of thought and word. It was a time before evil and good; a time before choosing. It was a time before light and darkness. And there was no thought or whisper or vision of the darkness to come. For these things were yet far off and of no substance or certainty.

There was peace and an eternal calm. But what calm and peace and joy there was would indeed be shaken, torn and broken by events never imagined or dreamed before this, the first of all beginnings.

Before all beginnings, he was. He was all and there was nothing apart from him. He was Yahweh. He was Elohim - the three in one.

Whether by voice and tongue or only by thought and purpose, Elohim spoke.

"Let there be."

The sound of his voice was deep and pure and strong and sweet. It was soft as a whisper, a feather in the breeze. It was warm as sunshine and clear as a crystal pool.

His words flowed like water and light from here to there. And there was elsewhere. His thoughts took shape and all the while, his voice swelled and echoed.

Now the words became great and countless, a never ending sea of words that flowed and took shape ever on the heals of "Let there be."

Such was the beginning, where passion fueled by will and purpose were drawn and held together in love and in the embrace of Elohim.

The thoughts of Elohim became substance and all his words moved outward and inward. And there was space and time. There was an endless creation with no limits, no walls or barriers. This would be the dwelling place of all things in creation.

So Elohim would dwell in space and beyond space and make his abode in time.

And time would know no end. Infinity and eternity were now in the hands of Elohim.

Though all creation had no end, greater was the creator whose endlessness was beyond the endlessness of creation. There was a here and there and elsewhere. And Elohim was in all. And the light of Elohim shone within and without and elsewhere.

Then Elohim said "Let there be."

And desire became words and words became substance. And in this new creation of space and time, Elohim would share love and give gifts. And the love of the father became gifts for the Son. And the love of the Son became gifts for the Spirit. Their love became gifts from one to all and all to one.

The voice of the Father spoke, "Let there be gifts and giving so that I might give my heart and share my love and my high and perfect thoughts."

And the Son echoed the one desire and said "Let there be, for my love shall be seen and known in everlasting gifts."

And the Spirit said, "Let there be. And let love be touched and seen and heard and held."

And Elohim created gifts of beauty, of colour and sound with shape and depth and height and breadth. The light of Elohim formed boundaries and walls and gates and pillars.

There came things of gold and sapphire and ruby and pearl but not of the kind to which man speaks and desires. They were of surpassing beauty. These things became ever weaved together, the onyx and that which resembled ivory unmarred, and all precious stones and substances. But unlike paler reflections in the realm of man, they were made, in part, of light; and light was in them and the light shone around them.

And gifts of living spirit things emerged from the light of Elohim. And grass and tree and river and lake and flower took shape.

There was a land of spirit and light with walls and halls and paths and lakes and trees. All beautiful things beyond imagination adorned the walls and halls and pathways.

And there was in the midst of the land a citadel created by Elohim as a gift from one to all and all to one. Shining towers and pillars rose all around the sanctuary. Its roof was open to the translucent sky. Living, growing things melded with stone and precious metal and gem to form walls high to the edge of sight. A glow of soft golden light filled the hall expanding the vast array of colour that was in everything. Growing plants and vines with flowers and blossoms hung throughout. Silken-like curtains billowed in a gentle breeze as they draped down and across the walls and flew from the top of spires.

This was the citadel of Elohim.

In this citadel were fountains of water that were more than water but of spirit and light. The water was sweet to smell and a music rose from the fountains. The fountains were linked together by canals which channeled their way from the fountains into a pristine lake; a great sea, clear as crystal, bright and blue. And at the end of this Crystal Sea was a great hall as if for gathering. Beyond the hall was a raised throne; not like the throne of man or a King of the Earth.

Elohim was pleased as he saw before him a vast land and city shaped and carved by the will and words of Father, Son and Spirit.

Then Elohim said, "I shall take a form and a presence for all my purposes that for all eternity eyes might see and ears might hear. I shall be in all and above all and beyond all, but I shall be here and move there and go within and stand without. I shall take a form and sit upon my throne and walk upon my paths and all my purposes will be accomplished in this place."

And Elohim called this land of spirit and light "Heaven." And the citadel of Elohim was the heart of Heaven.

Now Elohim took form and clothed himself in radiant light and the light was Elohim. He was in Heaven and beyond Heaven and in creation but beyond all creation. Elohim was here and there and elsewhere.

Then Elohim sat upon his high throne in the heart of Heaven and proclaimed, "I am. I am the first and the last; the beginning and the end. I am and I will ever be. And all these things shall never pass away because I am and always will be."

And the love of Elohim could be touched and seen and heard but there were as yet none to hear, nor see, nor touch.

Then Elohim who sat upon the throne said, "Let there be gifts of act and service, of deed and of valor."

Elohim held out his hand and taking water from the Crystal Lake breathed on the water as it spilled from his hand. The water took shape as the breath of Elohim moved within the water. The light from Elohim's hand reflected throughout the water as it flowed to the stone floor before the throne. And the water took shape and the shape was as Elohim, a shadow of the form which Elohim took upon himself.

And Elohim said to the form; "You are Michael. For you are like to myself and a gift to me and from me. My life and love is my gift to you. You shall be my valiant one, the guardian of Heaven and beyond. And in you is but a portion of my strength. It shall be enough. A flaming sword of justice shall you don at your side in service to all that is good and right. May you never employ it. In this your strength, you shall bring peace for you are ever the defender of love and life. You shall be called a Prince of angels and rule with me for the accomplishment of all my purposes. My strength shall always be in you and my heart shall you always seek. My face shall you always desire and my words shall you always heed."

And Elohim instructed Michael to dip his hand into the sea and cast the water into the air of Heaven. As Michael did so, Elohim breathed life into the water of light as it scattered through the great hall in the throne room of Elohim. The drops became a driving rain swirling about the great hall and over the Crystal Lake. And the drops of water took shape as life entered them. They became living beings of light and spirit. And the first angels were birthed. A great host of angels stood before Elohim while many rose above the floor of the great hall.

Elohim spoke to all the host and said, "Serve your master Michael well as he serves me in all my bidding. He is your Prince and shepherd and you are his sheep and his brethren."

Now Elohim dipped his hand into the Lake a second time and breathed upon the water in his hand. And as life and light filled and flowed through the growing, changing form of the water, Elohim birthed a brother to Michael of like form and image.

And Elohim said, "You are Gabriel. You are my left hand and Prince of the angels. You shall be my messenger and my voice. You shall know my heart and all my ways and no thing will I withhold from you. For your voice shall be my voice and your words my words. You are my herald, a bearer of truth and promise. You shall serve me as a gift from Elohim; Father to Son and Son to Spirit. And this is my gift to you that you should see and know the great I AM. My wisdom shall be in you. My face shall you always desire and my words shall you always heed. You are my servant true but you shall rule at my side this Heaven."

Elohim instructed Gabriel to stretch his hand out to take the waters of Heaven's Lake. Elohim breathed his spirit into the waters and yet again, a host of angels found life and purpose.

Now there were in Heaven myriads of angels though no two were alike. Although individually unique, there were sorts or breeds, divisions and ranks. And though unique, they were bound together by similar traits and purposes.

All angels were of spirit but with different forms. Some were grand and imposing. Others were less in stature. All angels shone from a light within that could ebb and flow at will though never by their wills be diminished. For their light was the life of Elohim breathed into them at their making.

Angels were masters of the air and sky of Heaven and could move across it and through it at great speeds. Though not all angels were winged, all could fly and hover where they wished. Angels in appearance wore bright cloaks of white. These were garments of light, of angel kind, that could not be donned or discarded. Unlike the garb of man, they could not be grasped or torn but were a part of the form and body of angels fashioned by the light that burned within them and around them.

Michael's host were different in appearance than Gabriel's. They stood taller with greater breadth and girth. Their hair was darker and shorter. Their garments of bright white were yet not as white but noticeably paler and duller. They reflected like silver and bronze and were taut across their bodies giving the appearance of a metallic armor of light.

All bore wings though not needed for flight. The wings of angels, like their garments, were part of their forms and unlike those of other winged creatures were neither feather nor bone nor sinew. They were of spirit and light, and moved not like the flapping of bird's wings; but in flight, they hung gracefully in the air like billowing silk as if to catch the currents and drafts of Heaven's sky.

And like the intermittent light that shone through angel flesh and garment, the appearance of wings could as well subside at will or be manifest in full rigor, bold and vivid.

Gabriel's legions appeared more graceful and delicate. Though there was no lack or absence of strength and power. Their robes of light were whiter, more full and fluid, draped gracefully about their beings. They moved like a wisp of smoke in a gentle breeze. Not all had wings. Some had translucent trains like fine linen that gracefully trailed behind them in flight.

Now Michael was, as his host, armored in light and had wings that rose high and proud above him in flight. His eyes burned with flame and yet were soothing to look upon. Gabriel's eyes were deep and blue as the Crystal Lake in the heart of Heaven. Gabriel was without wings but shone whiter and brighter than all others. Both were grand and magnificent in their own respects and were preeminent beyond the forms of all others. For they were Archangels, and the very highest of that rank. They were the covering ones, keepers of Heaven's flock and guardians of Elohim's gates. They were the chosen ones, the shining ones and principal commanders of Heaven's host.

Michael, Gabriel and the angels sat long before the throne of Elohim in awe of all he was. As they were in his presence, Elohim imparted to them the mysteries of Heaven but only to Gabriel did he share the secret designs of his heart. And Gabriel knew all the mind of Elohim in so much as his form could hold.

And Michael stood at the right hand of Elohim while Gabriel stood at his left and they called him Adonai for he was their Lord and King. They took delight in his words and found joy in his presence and his bidding was their one desire. For Michael and Gabriel were the perfect ones, the anointed servants and yet little less than Kings of angels. And Michael and Gabriel were friends and true brothers. Each were gifted in unique fashion for the purposes of their King. And each would seek out the other to find unity and balance desiring to hear and learn from each other.

They both hungered and longed for, and were yet contented with, the joy and peace of Heaven. They could have never imagined how fragile contentment could be. For there were yet tears spilled, nor hearts broken nor swords drawn. And Elohim's heart was that it would always be so for these princes and sons. But time would turn all. And Heaven would ache for these early days of innocence.

2

The Foretelling

One day, far beyond the outer courts of the King, Michael was walking in the midst of the Garden in the east of Heaven. His mind was full of wonder. His heart was that of an explorer and all of Heaven was at his feet. Knowledge was a treasure to him and his hunger to know and discover was strong. With each new discovery a more than satisfactory bliss filled his heart.

Michael loved this realm called Heaven. He never tired of seeking and exploring. What joy there was for him in the finding of new treasures. And with every discovery, every puzzle, there was a new glimpse of the King of Heaven.

One day while in a deep recess of the garden, he came upon Gabriel who lay prostrate upon the grass and moss of the garden floor. Gabriel lay in quiet staring into the sky of Heaven which shone bright in a diffused variance of colour and light. The sky in Heaven was always changing and one moment it was as a wondrous painting blanketing the sky; clear and bright full of form and colour, but the next, it was a different work of art altogether. Gabriel in times of rest and refreshing would stare into the divergent canvas of the ever shifting sky. There he too found an endless joy in the beauty and diversity of Elohim's handiwork.

When Michael saw Gabriel his heart leapt within him at the sight of his friend and brother. For Michael loved Gabriel and thought always high of him.

"Greetings my brother and friend," said Michael. "What a joy and surprise to find you here in this small garden when all of Heaven is before you and its breadth and height is so great."

Gabriel was equally pleased and rising to his feet greeted him with an embrace, saying;

"What brings you Prince of Angels to this place to disrupt my meditation? And you are a pleasant disruption indeed. For seeing you here in this hidden corner of Heaven elevates my soul's rest to joy and laughter. For I was in quiet pondering all that has been shown to me and all that I see. Your presence is a welcome surprise."

"I was but wandering and had no idea that I would find you here" said Michael.

"Come, my brother," said Gabriel. "Let us walk and talk together in this garden far away from the zeal and passion stirring in the heart of Heaven. What is it my friend that fills your thoughts?"

Michael spoke softly and slowly. "I often take these times to think and meditate and to gaze into every corner. For who knows what shall meet me there in these hidden places? And without exception, there is always a wonder. And with every wonder a puzzle to solve. And with every answer there are more questions.

Gabriel, my brother, there are so many mysteries without and questions within. And so I seek. And in seeking such great wonders I always find, or perhaps they find me. My hunger satisfied turns to joy – an ever increasing joy. I am full and happy. But then I turn a corner, cross a river, peer into a hidden grotto or rise to the roof of Heaven and am met always with a new wonder, an undiscovered marvel and so too a new hunger to birth a new joy. I love to learn of these things but the more I learn, it seems the more I am in need of learning.

When I discover something new, yesterday's joy becomes a memory. Today's joy is unequaled. And yet I know that tomorrow's joy will surpass today's. All and everything reflects the heart of Elohim. And though I stand daily in his presence, I feel as close and full when I am here in his creation."

Gabriel laughed a little.

Michael continued, giving Gabriel little room for more than a nod and an approving "Aye."

"When I walk these gardens or rise to the very edge of Heaven, I see his heart and love and passion more clearly. For it seems to me that such beauty is born in a heart of one far more beautiful."

"It is a gift, mine as well as yours," said Gabriel.

Michael wondered aloud, "Do you my brother seek such knowledge as do I? For surely you are his second mind and he fills you with all his knowledge."

"This is true in part my brother," answered Gabriel. "For in my keeping Elohim has shared his dreams and plans in part, but not all is mine. It could not be so, for my thoughts are not his. I am a vessel into which the secrets of Heaven are poured. But you too are his chosen one and to you has been granted equally the secrets of Heaven."

Michael responded; "You are his most trusted servant."

"Not so my brother," said Gabriel. "I am not so far beyond your knowledge. For you grow according to your hunger. You are a seeker and adventurer, a doer of deeds and a conqueror of dreams. You seek the treasure of knowledge and he is delighted to guide you to your journey's end.

As for me, I too hunger, but not with such eagerness as you. And what knowledge I do have, I keep in secret for times yet to be declared."

Gabriel leapt onto a small hill and turned to Michael. "In service to him, at his bidding, I will divulge my mind and herald mysteries that I still do not fully grasp myself."

Michael leapt to his side.

"And so my dear friend," Gabriel continued while stretching his arm around Michael's shoulder, "we are the same and yet different. What you hunger for, you discover richly. What I know is whispered in my ear. We both know his mind - each in part. And brother, lest you feel I am in a privileged place; I have need to learn from you."

Michael's heart glowed at such tribute from the wisest of Heaven's Princes and turning his head away glanced around the garden with a childlike innocence.

"There are mysteries I see only a glimpse of and riddles that I shall never uncover. My angel eyes can see to the edge of Heaven but not beyond. I wonder Gabriel, what more is there beyond my vision? There must be more. I am sure. Or perhaps there is more yet to come. Perhaps Elohim is not finished with creation."

"You are wise my brother;" responded Gabriel, "for you see well beyond your angel eyes. All mysteries shall unfold in time, but the story of Heaven and creation is just begun. You see and imagine correctly. There is indeed more."

Michael's eyes opened wide.

"Gabriel, is this true? Is there more to this Heaven than my eyes have seen? For it seems to me that I have walked every path and climbed every hill. Is there a sea or river in which I have not dipped my hand? Where can I turn to see more? I know that Heaven is a growing, living place. As grand and great as this is, there must be more. Is it so? Is there more Gabriel?"

Michael closed his eyes for a moment before continuing. "I cannot see beyond the walls of Heaven.

Still what can there be beyond its borders and gates? Whether here or there or yet to come, I long to know it, if indeed there is anything to know."

Gabriel nodded his head and pausing for a time replied; "Beyond the borders of this realm there is nothing. It is an empty canvas, white and pure. But a brush rests idle in Elohim's hand for a time. Very soon Elohim will set brush to canvas and we shall see a new creation."

Michael stood erect and his heart came to attention. His eyes focused intently on Gabriel and standing amazed he asked; "Do you know of these mysteries? Can you tell me Gabriel, what is yet to come?"

"My eager brother," said Gabriel with a half laugh; "I do and can. For there is no thing which he desires hidden from us. But what is hidden is simply yet to be discovered or yet to be revealed. All knowledge and all mysteries are held by him with open hands that we might know and understand in our own time. And though I may gain the knowledge first, it is equally for you to know."

Gabriel reached out his hand and gently gripped Michael's shoulders and almost apologetically, he continued; "I can share only in part for I know only in part. Today we have a glimpse, one day it shall be for all to see and understand."

"Tell me my truest friend" urged Michael, "all that you know and all that you suppose."

Gabriel sat again in the grass and leaning upon a tree, gestured to Michael to sit beside him. As Michael sat, Gabriel began. "There is a world to come as vast as all we know in and beyond the gates of Heaven. But it is a lesser world, still of beauty and majesty. This world is now in the heart of Elohim and will soon come to pass, but it is a world more frail than this place in which we dwell. It is of a substance we do not know that can bend and break at will. It will be a world of fragile order held together by Elohim's hand."

"Frail and fragile? How can this be Gabriel?" Michael interrupted. "For there is nothing fragile about Elohim's hand."

Gabriel continued. "This world as I understand, and my vision is not so clear as we would both like, will be held also in other hands less sure than Elohim's. Elohim himself will entrust this creation to others dear to him. It will be a gift and inheritance for ones who shall possess and rule this new creation."

"Now my heart truly burns. I cannot imagine such a place." Michael hesitated. "And I know no hands worthy of such a gift. Whose hands are these Gabriel? Shall angels yet to come have such an inheritance?"

"Calm, my brother" encouraged Gabriel, raising his hand as if to slow Michael.

"You shall know all my mind concerning these things. It is not angels I speak of, though there shall also come other beings of angel kind. Yes, there shall be other beings of great beauty and perfection and Heaven shall be their home. But these are not of whom I speak.

The coming ones shall not be as we are, for we are angel kind made of spirit and light. We are fit for this world as servants of the most high and in all this we are made happy. But there are those yet to come upon whom Elohim's eyes and heart are set."

Michael continued to question Gabriel. "What kind of beings are these who will hold such in their hands? Brother, my mind is stretched and all my heart is bursting."

Gabriel gathered his thoughts "I know only this that they shall be Elohim's gift of love one to another - Father to Son, Son to Spirit, all to all. They shall be lesser beings of greater worth."

"Are we too not gifts of love from Elohim to Elohim?" queried Michael.

"This we are," said Gabriel. "For we are made by love and we declare and proclaim his love. Our service, our work, our deeds are an expression of love. And we too are partakers of that very great love. But the coming ones will be gifts of love and intimacy and friendship. For when their time is full, they will fully join in the embrace of Elohim."

"How can this be?" asked Michael. "How can that which is not Elohim be so joined to Elohim? How can creation unite so with the creator?"

"Because, and this is the greatest mystery, they shall be his children true; the offspring and beloved children of Elohim."

"Are we not his children and do we not call him Father? He loves us and we love him," proclaimed Michael.

Gabriel carefully chose his words. "We are truly his children as he has birthed us. We love him and he loves us. But we too are his servants crafted to serve. Love is our reward but not our purpose. Those who will come are crafted to love and to know love without measure. They will be fashioned in his image. They will be sons and daughters to the Father. They will be sisters and brothers to the Son. And they will be the people of the Spirit. And the Spirit will forever dwell not apart but within these children of Elohim."

A happy tear rolled down Michael's cheek as he thought long of what these beings might be. Though he did not grasp it, he could see some great purpose in Elohim's plan. Something in his heart was overjoyed and yet overwhelmed.

"What mysteries! What marvels!" he said. "Of these things, I cannot imagine though my heart is full of expectation. Gabriel, will they be so different than us for are we not created in his image?"

"Yes my brother, we are in part;" said Gabriel, whose heart was equally full at the telling as was Michael's at the hearing. "But these coming ones are a shadow of his being. They shall be created in his image by his own hand for the highest of all his purposes; for endless intimacy with Elohim."

Ever wanting more clarity, Michael continued his pursuit of detail, "Tell me more Gabriel. Tell me all."

"I can say little more than I have said," spoke Gabriel. "So shall I again echo what I know.

You and I are creatures of light and exist to do his will. We are free to do so. But in the doing of his will is our destiny fulfilled.

And to what end do we exist? Ages hence, our deeds and doings, our service and our valor can be counted and our purpose shall be measured, for we exist for the doing and love is our reward and great pleasure.

But the value of the coming ones is not in their deeds and service to Elohim. If no deeds and service were ever measured and counted, still would Elohim take joy in the children he has birthed and in the fellowship and friendship forged with them. Their being is enough.

Though the embrace of Elohim is complete and lacking nothing, still Elohim has purposed that they partake of his embrace forever. They are gifts from Elohim to Elohim - not of service but of intimacy as none other shall ever know. They are, and will be through all ages, children created but for one purpose - to be children. And they shall ever know kinship with the great I Am."

"What manner of beings are these? And when shall we see them? I long to see such a thing, for that which brings joy to Elohim is my greatest joy," Michael sighed.

"I do not know my brother," said Gabriel "but we are the first. They shall be the last. And we shall forever see the wonder of the children of Elohim; for they shall shine forth as a great sun of light, even in a small way as Elohim himself."

Now Michael and Gabriel spoke long concerning the coming children of Elohim. And in their hearts they loved them before they were birthed and wanted only to see them and serve them and call them friends.

Now a great gathering of all who dwelt in Heaven stood in the great hall at the bidding of Elohim; all creatures great and small. Michael and Gabriel stood at Elohim's right and left. There was a great noise of singing and clapping of hands and shouting in the hall of halls. A thousand songs with ten thousand voices blended together and echoed through the whole of Heaven and beyond.

Then Michael and Gabriel raised their hands before the throng and all fell silent. All eyes beheld the face of the Father of all creation.

Then together in one voice and one great harmony, Elohim spoke; "Let there be gifts of praise, of music, of song and singing. Let there be gifts of worship and honor and tribute."

And for a third time, Elohim dipped his hand into the Crystal Lake and breathed upon the water as it sank to the floor. And form and shape took hold of the water as the spirit and life of Elohim came into the water. Now standing before the host of Heaven was a being and creature unlike any eyes had seen or any mind could imagine. Such was the beauty of this being that all hearts melted before it and angels cried out in unison, "Great is Elohim."

Now this being looked at first similar to the form with which Elohim clothed himself, less in size and splendor but almost equal in brightness, as the light which shone in this being, as in Michael and Gabriel, shone all the brighter at his birth. And when angel eyes could adjust and see beyond the subsiding brightness of that new creation, a marvelous and wonderful being was uncovered. Unlike the flowing white silk and linen or the shining gold and silver of other angels, his garment of light seemed like that of precious stone of which there was no equal in all of Heaven. And upon the cloak of light that was his tent were numerous instruments hung like swords. These instruments were for the playing, for music and song. His eyes were of a colour never seen before in Heaven and his hair shone as bright as the train of Elohim.

Elohim spoke to the form. "You are Lucifer, my chosen one, perfect and more beautiful than all beings and creatures in all creation. You are the anointed one to whom I have given the greatest gift. You will sing and make melody and harmony and symphony as has never been heard in all of Heaven. And the music and words of my heart you shall bring to Elohim from Elohim as a herald of my great love. You are to me and from me a gift of music and praise, of worship and honor and reverence.

You shall be the creator of beauty seen by the eyes, held by hands, sung from hearts and heard with the ears. You are the joy bringer who stands before the throne. You shall speak the heart of Father, Son and Spirit and all to all. And my love you shall declare to all creation as you ever gaze upon the embrace of Elohim.

Our passion and our delight you shall see and know. Then you shall proclaim all my esteem and my heart's affection. For you are Lucifer, Prince of angels. And you shall seek my heart all your days and do my bidding to your heart's delight. And to you I give the greatest of all gifts, to stand before me and to witness the love and passion of Elohim. And this gift shall fuel your gift of music and art and worship. All of Heaven will sing your songs, delight in your worship and revel in your beauty and the creation of your heart and hands."

Lucifer bowed before the throne. Then Elohim instructed Lucifer to dip his hands into the Lake of Crystal to take from it. And as before, Elohim breathed his spirit and life into the water held in Lucifer's hands and such was born a great host of creatures who now filled the great hall of the King before the throne of Elohim. And these creatures shone brighter and rose higher in flight than all others and hovered around the throne.

Then Lucifer rose to the highest point in the Temple of Elohim and his light grew brighter and brighter. As the music began to flow and grow, the host flew to and fro from one side of the great hall to beyond the Lake. Streaks of brilliant colour and vaporous splashes followed the angel's dance. Tinted markings and painted trails of light; symbols and script flashed across the sky. And the sound of diverse musical instruments was everywhere, played skillfully by perfect hands from perfect hearts. The sky became a canvas full of images and paintings; of light and colour. And together with all his host, Lucifer sang a song and played a symphony that rang throughout all of Heaven. A feast of sound and light filled all of Elohim's realm.

Michael and Gabriel marveled for they could not imagine a music greater than that which had been known and daily filled Heaven and which daily rose from the fountains and which daily flowed from the mouths of angels. Even the song of their own heart was pale in comparison. Never was the voice of angels so pure and a song so sweet. The words of the throng were high and exalted proclaiming the love and the majesty of Elohim. And the Father delighted with the praises offered for the Son. Spirit and Son beamed with joy at the magnificence of the Father portrayed in symphony, in colour and in script. The greatness of his love and heart were so utterly declared in word and song and light.

This was indeed a happy day for Heaven. And for an age, the angels all joined in, abandoning their charges to rapture before the throne of Heaven.

In all of Heaven, Lucifer was a marvel. And Michael and Gabriel embraced Lucifer and called him friend and brother. They loved him true as he loved them.

Now Gabriel sat at the left hand of Elohim and Michael's place of honor was at the right of Elohim's throne though duty took them to the ends of Heaven as commanders of the host. But Lucifer's place was ever before the throne. His host, over which he was Archangel, commander, and Lord, were all about the throne offering their gifts to Elohim.

The work of Lucifer's hand adorned the halls and walls of Heaven for he was ever creating that of beauty. He was an artist and craftsman with no equal and a peerless musician and a master of words and of script. In the ancient symbols and words of angels, his poetry was engraved on the walls of the great hall.

He used all the precious stone in Heaven; fine and pure metals, crystals and substances half light and half jewel shaping and molding them by his will and hands alone. And many great stones shaped and carved in forms of such splendor decorated the gardens from one end of Heaven to another. His art he taught to many. All his knowledge and skill were but a gift and shadow of the craft of Elohim. His work brought great joy to Elohim and all of Heaven.

Now Gabriel and Michael shared all they knew of the coming ones with Lucifer who marveled as did they. And Lucifer wondered much in his heart of these and many other mysterious things. He was an artist who fueled his mind with imagination. And skillfully created whatever his heart could imagine. In his imaginations, he wondered much of what these coming children of Elohim would be like. And together with Gabriel and Michael they would discuss what might be.

3

The Threat of Malice

One day, Lucifer took Gabriel and Michael to the highest pinnacle of Heaven. From there, with angel eyes, they could see all of Heaven, from the Citadel of Elohim to the woods beyond the western plains and as far as the pillars of light that rose above the mountains on the far side of the northern glens. These pillars marked the borders of the kingdom of Elohim beyond which was endlessness.

"What majesty is in this place," said Lucifer.

"And you in part have made it so," said Michael.

"It is a canvas which I long to cover," responded Lucifer. "And I have so imagined new wonders as to make all hearts glad."

"You are the shining one," said Gabriel. "Elohim has made you higher and greater and more pleasing to the eye than all else."

"And so I am," said Lucifer, "not by my own making but by his hand alone. For I and you with me are the measure of his heart and desire. In us is seen his high art. We are privileged, we three, to be but small reflections of Elohim."

"Aye" said Michael. "We are wondrously made. But there are those coming of whom I can scarcely imagine. My heart wonders of what they shall be made and what kind of beings shall they truly be. For surely, they will be great if Elohim ordains it."

Lucifer responded, "Do you think they shall be like us in grace and beauty or in power and art?"

"And beyond;" said Gabriel, "The likes of which we can scarcely imagine. And yet not like us at all."

Lucifer turning full in the face of Gabriel asked, "But will they be as beautiful as I and will their music be as my own? And will they be more wise than you and will they have greater strength than Michael? On this my mind has dwelt long. For I cannot imagine they will be as we are. Different than we? Of this I am certain.

For what Elohim created in me is perfected and full without lack or want or equal. Can even Elohim create that which is beyond his highest? Can my perfection be less than perfect when the coming ones are revealed? I am the shining one. By his own voice I have heard this honor. Not of my own doing. This is only a gift to me and through me to all others. And tell me brothers, can there be one who shines brighter, for this is what I am and what he has made me to be?"

Lucifer hesitated and lifted his head to the sky as if lost in some distant imagination.

He continued; "It occurs to me my brothers; though I am truly perfect by his design and skill, as are you, still no one except our creator can know what I shall become in due course."

There was silence as both Gabriel and Michael pondered Lucifer's words for there was something that they could not grasp.

Gabriel spoke almost in a whisper. "What the coming ones will be is but a shadow for me. Elohim has kept this a great mystery for all of Heaven. But what I have heard and seen in the heart of Elohim leads me to believe that their surpassing value will be found in none of these things in which we marvel - neither beauty, nor music, nor skill, nor service.

We are gifts of service and honor and worship and valor. These coming ones will have great value but not in what they do. They are not gifts of service or works of any kind. It is clear to me that the greatest desire in the heart of Elohim is to bear children in his likeness for his joy and pleasure. And I sense that all of creation in Heaven and beyond eagerly anticipates the unveiling of his greatest creation - the coming ones. In this is their surpassing value, that they shall resemble their father who creates them by his own hand in his very likeness. And they are created for the very highest of all purposes to be his children forever."

"But Lucifer," continued Gabriel, "some of what you imagine is true indeed; for they shall I think not be like us neither in beauty or strength or knowledge and skill. I foresee that they shall be more frail and lowly in appearance for a time until all is fulfilled. And what they shall be is unclear to me."

Lucifer answered quickly with an excitement unbefitting the discussion. "No they shall not be like us nor can they ever be! You speak rightly my brother, for I too can foresee something of these coming ones. And I cannot imagine beings more than we; for there is unattainable perfection in we three Princes of Heaven. And if we are perfect now this day, then what shall we become tomorrow? No one yet knows what I shall become, but I am certain it is marvelous indeed."

Gabriel and Michael both again heard in Lucifer's words something which puzzled them but they remained silent and eager to hear from their brother.

Lucifer continued, "I perceive that the true nature of these coming ones is less than what Gabriel has imagined. Pardon me my brother. It's not that I doubt your sight or wisdom. But reason has led me to see another prospect.

Now hear my thoughts on this my brothers. Is there any like Gabriel whose wisdom is near to Elohim's?"

Lucifer turned to Michael and looked full into his face. Michael remained silent as was his habit during the many discussions they shared. Michael was one who measured his thoughts and spoke only when he felt confident in his deliberations.

Lucifer turning toward Gabriel stepped back to stand beside Michael reaching his arm around his shoulder. Now the two stood side by side facing Gabriel.

Lucifer continued; "We are Archangels who cover all. We serve Elohim as all else serves us. This is our post and position to rule at his side. Happy are we to do all his bidding as commanders of his entire host. And so should not the coming ones serve as well; for can we expect less of them? Does Elohim not deserve their service along with ours? Shall we not continue in our place of duty? No, I think these coming ones, as special as they are, will serve Elohim as all else and in serving will remain under our gentle command."

Lucifer pulled Michael closer to him shoulder to shoulder and said "In Michael's silence I have found a like mind and kindred heart."

He continued, "Is there or shall there ever be any with courage and strength and a heart as strong as Michael's?

I can read my brother well, for even now, he surely sees as I see. Michael, I am certain agrees with me in these trivial matters. In this, we are one and together."

Lucifer laughed just a little. "Surely this Prince is not made to serve a lesser being is he? For though my brother remains ever silent, he surely knows his worth."

Michael turned, breaking the half embrace and looking full into the face of Lucifer, spoke with a severity never heard or seen. For in all of Heaven through ages past, never was there provocation for stern words. But perfect hearts still beget uncertain dialogue. And it was more for clarity that Michael spoke.

Michael spoke slowly, firmly and deliberately.

"Do not, my brother, mistake my silence for ignorance or lack of attention to every word you utter. For deep is my deliberation and I shall speak my mind when I have reason to do so. Neither mistake my silence for accord. My thoughts are my own and they will go where I direct them. They do not follow you nor your imaginations. And when I speak my mind you shall hear it and know it beyond all doubt.

Where your thoughts now go, I do not know nor will I follow them. For true it is that we are great made by greater hands but we are what we are by his will and not that of our own. If he deems a greater work that shall in any way make us the lesser; then so be it, to his good and glory and pleasure. And should these coming ones be Kings, I shall serve with the same delight as I now rule."

Gabriel sensed the provocation in Michael's heart and turning to Lucifer with more gentle expressions still pursued his reasoning.

"My brother," said Gabriel, "what is it that you suppose you will become that you are not now and ever will be? Have we mistaken your intention? For I too am puzzled by the direction of your thoughts."

Lucifer was bewildered at the lack of accord in Michael and Gabriel. He could not understand how they were not yet in harmony with his wise verdict concerning the coming ones. He spoke to them now as if speaking to children in need of instruction.

"My brothers, whom I love as much as my own being, this discourse gives me opportunity to unfold my thoughts before you. And so in love and trust I will do so. Hear me now and consider with supple minds and open hearts what I am eager to share with you.

I am Heaven's artist. I am its great player and composer. I conduct Heaven's host. As such, I am privileged to be the creator of that which brings joy to all. And this could not be so except for my imaginations and speculations. I am, first of all, a dreamer. I dream of what might be; what could be. It is my gift to see what others cannot. And to this end does my gift have merit. I create from imagination works of beauty for all to cherish.

What I imagine, I see as though real. And in order to make it true and substantial, a sight for eyes and an object to hold, I set my will to make it so. And by the skill of my hands and the power within me, what my heart sees is brought into being - carried from the imaginations of my mind to certainty. This is the essence of my art.

My mind is a fertile womb which nurtures and births the substantial from the seeds of inspiration. This is my gift to dream and create. And what I create is for Elohim and all of Heaven.

But how can you truly grasp this, for your gifts have no need of such a fertile imagination as mine? And so I understand the reason for your questioning. But your questions are built on a lack of knowledge. This is not to your own fault, for there is no fault in such perfection. But he has made you for other purposes than I. And my gift is to imagine; for there is no art or poetry or created beauty unless the heart and mind can foresee it.

And as my art is a living, growing thing moving ever toward greater perfection, so am I. I too grow and expand and will become more than I am now in time. And I am not what I shall be. He has created in me a gift that grows to be more than at first and is now less than it will be. For much greater will the fruit of my mind and work of my hands be in time to come. Can you not see the great pleasure I bring to Elohim in my music and worship? And so will I not become all the greater to bring him greater gifts and greater pleasure?"

Lucifer lifted his arms and waved them about toward all of Heaven around them.

"That which you have just now admired, which adorns the halls of Heaven, could never be unless first my heart could imagine it. And of course I will imagine greater things than these. I too am a creator. My gift is my sight and my imagination. To perform such wonders I must be able to envision what is not, what is yet to exist. Then, with all my strength and skill, I will it into being to his benefit and all of Heaven. And so brothers, I am a seer and a doer as well. My fertile imagination and my determined will bring from nothing, something of great worth."

Gabriel and Michael had no response. They were truly trying to understand their friend and brother.

Lucifer continued, "I too can see and imagine something of the coming ones; of what they will be and might ever be. And my imaginations are more substantial than you might think; for they are more a vision of the future than just misty dreams. Listen and take heed of these visions from one who creates wonders with such visions.

It is unthinkable that the coming ones shall ever be beyond what we are or what I shall become. And what I shall become is more and greater than I am now. Not that I desire it, for I can only walk the path Elohim has chosen for me. And this is his will that there be none greater in eminence or stature than his covering angels. What he loves in us today, he will love all the more tomorrow for there shall be more to love.

How can there be greater than we, when Elohim has ordained our greatness and our perfection? And to the utter heights of all his purposes I will rise; for he has created in me a destiny to which no one can aspire."

Gabriel un-at-ease spoke, "I see my brother that you have pondered long about what the coming ones shall be, but perhaps even more about what you shall be. Friend, I cannot question your design and purpose nor your destiny. But of the coming ones Elohim has imparted to me things not imagined but spoken. And true it is that he has perfected in you a gift of great and limitless value. But I have in part seen the heart of Elohim. What he intends is beyond our counsel and imaginations.

Though you can see what is not, your gift of imagination is only for the creating and by that design you have only what skill he has placed in you. You do not know the boundaries of your imaginations and skills and powers. Still, boundaries there are. But his skill has no limits and what he imagines is higher and greater than all of his creation. And though he delights in the beings we are, there is to come greater still. And if he wills it, they shall surpass that which he birthed in us. His delight in us will never diminish and yet how slight are we in his greatness."

Gabriel drew close to Lucifer. Standing face to face, he stretched out both of his hands and affectionately grasped Lucifer's upper arms. Looking straight into his eyes he said, "And now hear my concern brother. If Elohim deems us great, we have no need to proclaim it more loudly. And what he determines to be greater still will be so by his power and will and love."

Michael rose above the two and hovered for a time before announcing, "I am summoned."

He greatly desired to stay as he felt some warning in his heart. The warning grew to a discomfort he had never known. His desire was to protect but from what, he did not know. For though his instinct was that of a protector and warrior, there was never a cause for such in Heaven. His heart stirred beyond his understanding. He wished he could watch silently over this discourse to which he was little more than a spectator. But go he must, for the Spirit of Elohim was calling to him. He left and flew in haste toward the Citadel of Elohim.

Michael reached the citadel of Elohim in flight and rested a few meters from the flame above the throne. He bowed his head as he approached. "Adonai," he said, "I am your servant."

"And my son as well," said the voice from the throne.

"Have you need of me my Lord?"

"No need my son," spoke Elohim. "But you have need of me to calm a fever that rises in your angel blood."

Michael hastily replied, "Yes I feel it Father. In the garden just now, it rose within me like a terrible fountain."

"Do not be alarmed at this," said Elohim. "For you are built for action and valor as well as love. This day, I keep you from action too swift. I have brought you here now to slow and soothe your heart."

Michael fell to his knees. He looked up to the figure of Elohim who stood in the midst of the fire. With quivering voice ill-befitting his strength he whispered; "Something burns within me Father but I do not know what or why. But now in your presence it is quenched."

"Michael," spoke Elohim. "You are Heaven's guardian and more. In you are the eyes and ears of a skilled hunter who sees his prey stirring at a great distance. And though none others see the movement, you are prepared to draw your bow and strike.

You are a watcher on the wall who by nature and duty keeps vigilant from a strong tower in order to protect your home from all threats. You are stirred because of what you see in the distance. But the alarm in you may be for naught. For what you see may be little more than dust stirred by the wind. Keep watch my son, but do not act. Be wary but leave your sword sheathed until the threat is real and upon you."

"Father, you know and hear all," said Michael. "You know beyond the words spoken today in the garden between friends and brothers. If this is true that I am a warrior trained to stand and fight; then is it not inevitable that this will come to no good end? Tell me Father; is this your destiny for me, to battle? For I hate the very word and notion."

"My son," replied Elohim, "what do you know of battle or quarrel?"

"Nothing my Lord. It is but a concept. I see it all around me.

It is in the wind that blows against what will not be moved. Trees stand and bend and leaves fall and fail while the relentless wind contests with the forests of Heaven. I can see that light pushes back darkness and when the light subsides, the darkness moves in to win the day until the light comes again in strength to take back what is lost. This is quarrel. It is everywhere. The river quarrels with the river bed. The creatures of Heaven quarrel as well; birds with the sky, sea creatures with the currents.

But this I have never seen heart to heart or will to will – not in angel kind. This is battle is it not? And I fear Father that I feel it in my bones.

My Lord and maker, my heart desires peace and finds unrest at the thought of quarrel. Father answer me this, am I but a sword and shield prepared to strike against those whom I would rather love? Is this your design for me?"

"My valiant warrior; and this you are," said Elohim; "you are strong with gentle heart. And it is your heart not your strength that brings me joy. Your purpose is not to battle but to serve and love whom you serve. Neither battle nor service is of any value without the love.

Strength and courage are yours my faithful one. But you are not a weapon in my hand. Nor have I set a course of conflict for you or your brothers. What you hate, I hate the more and what you love, I love the more. You are indeed able to stand against the most violent wind; but I do not will or want that even a gust would sore your eyes.

A bird is built for flight and because of such can withstand a fall from the highest heights. But it is not built for the falling. In like manner, you are prepared to do what neither of us could ever desire."

Michael stood erect before Elohim and said "If my understanding is true, Father, that which agitates my heart is in no way a certainty and my fevered senses are but a warning of what might never come and need not be. Do I speak truth Father?"

"Yes, Michael, you see it very well," said Elohim. "The end of this day is not yet written. But what is inevitable is that, in my realm, love is given not taken. And it can only be given if the heart has freedom to withhold it. If love is withheld, then a violent wind will indeed strike all of Heaven and you my son are prepared to stand. You are built to fly not to fall. Now wait and rest here a while with me my son. Think not of what has or will transpire, for you cannot aid Gabriel in the speaking of wisdom. Nor can you steer the drifting of reason in Lucifer's heart. Gabriel will speak for me."

4

The First Debate

Gabriel wished Michael had stayed by his side as his presence always brought comfort. And now that comfort would be most welcome. But Michael was gone and might not return before this dialogue was complete. Gabriel mustered his attention to hear and respond to the twisted reason that assaulted his mind.

"My brother Michael shall come to clarity in these things," said Lucifer. "For he is perfect and wise and thoughtful. And he shall know that in innocence I imagine and wonder. And of what importance is it if I imagine wrongly. For all is but conjecture, prospect and possibilities, all without substance or error. Nor can these thoughts and speculations be anything but submitted to Elohim's greater purposes."

Lucifer in his own mind now became the teacher, seeing Gabriel as in need of such.

He gestured to Gabriel to sit on the ground before him. Gabriel said nothing and chose to stand instead.

Lucifer continued, "As in the art that adorns Heaven, there is never a finished work. The artist begins with a longing that can never truly be satisfied. It is the nature of inspiration. Never is the work finished, but always abandoned. Perfection is a shifting thing not easily grasped. And when one pursues perfection, it will forever be just beyond his reach. For always is there room for a deeper colour; a different stroke, an addition of form and style; a slight alteration. Even the most skilled hands cannot catch or capture the ever growing and changing notion of the artist.

In the thousands of forms and pictures I have fashioned, I have yet to complete one. But before one is perfect and complete to my full satisfaction, my heart is drawn to another. And so it is with imaginations, Gabriel. There is no error and no offence in my imaginations; only innocence. They are ever growing speculations of little import until they reach their end. They are but unfinished works in my mind and should be of little consequence to the hearer."

Part of Gabriel thought this reasonable as he trusted still his brother Lucifer.

"But surely, there are things of which our hearts cannot or should not imagine" said Gabriel.

"I think not;" said Lucifer. "For that which a perfect mind conjures is indeed perfect. It is only in the doing that perfection fails. But to think it and dream it; this is always profitable. There are no thoughts that cannot be birthed in our perfect minds. And that which is only in our minds has no substance to vex our hearts."

Lucifer drew closer to Gabriel as if to whisper, though there was no need to do so, and said, "I shall tell you my deepest imagination though Michael may not ever comprehend it fully. But you and I are not like him. He is one for action and valor and our deliberations may be too deep for him as yet. But you Gabriel in your wisdom shall see the pleasure and innocence in such a whimsy."

Gabriel more at ease sat down to listen.

Lucifer now towering above his brother felt sure he would woo and win Gabriel's deeper affection and greater support.

He began again; "As I have long stood before the throne of Elohim and marveled at him, for nothing has he kept from me, I have imagined what it would be like to be like Elohim. I have wondered long in this regard. What would it be like to be the creator of all and the source of all; the commander of all? I have further wondered as I present my great gifts to him, how full and complete is his heart at the receiving of such gifts; such honor and love. He ordains great beings to do great things all for his pleasure. How marvelous!

Though I delight now in the creating and giving, I think greater than the giver is the one who receives. What joy to be as Elohim and what honor and glory to sit on his throne before the adoring host of Heaven to be loved and served and worshipped by all.

And Gabriel have you ever in innocence wondered such? What would it be like to be as Elohim or his equal in power and majesty and glory?"

"Never!" said Gabriel briskly standing to his feet. "And I can see no pleasure in thinking so. Whether innocent or not, it seems that this imagination can have no purpose that serves the King of Heaven."

A look of surprise came to Lucifer's face. His glowing eyes narrowed as if truly shocked by the forcefulness of Gabriel's answer.

"And in this you are as Michael," he said half laughing. "Do you not know that there could be no greater honor than to desire to be like another; and no less honor to imagine it? For I have also imagined what it would be like to be as you. My love and honor is manifested in these imaginations. They are a tribute to Elohim and this he knows as my heart is ever for him."

Gabriel was mystified at Lucifer's words and yet marveled in his wisdom. And within his heart, Gabriel questioned his own response and lack of understanding. He listened more intently.

Lucifer continued; "And do you not understand Elohim's plan and design for me Gabriel? He has created me to dream in order to bring life to that very dream. There can be nothing but pure innocence in the wonder, especially when the wonder honors him so. For hardly would one dream of walking in the steps of a lesser being. It is because I honor his greatness that I wonder so."

Gabriel still puzzled asked; "And how is it that you set your compass toward fantasies that can never come to life? What in this is purpose and fulfillment, to dream what you cannot do, or create, or bring to life? For you can never be as Elohim. And do you not also wonder Lucifer, if in the wondering, you have brought him pleasure? Is he pleased by such imaginations as these; you Lucifer, dreaming of being like Elohim without hope of ever becoming so?"

As if correcting an angel of lesser rank, Lucifer responded; "I set my compass to that which I deem good and agreeable and I am free to do so. And because he has given me this freedom, the use of it must bring him pleasure. If I deny this gift then I would truly cause him alarm.

Gabriel be reasonable. There is no injury to Elohim in the thinking and dreaming when there can never be the doing."

Lucifer paused and gathering his thoughts continued; "And even if the dream could be accomplished and I could be as Elohim, has he not shown himself to be one who shares all that is his to share? And in his great love and humility, would he ever strive with any for equality or recognition? His preeminence is not threatened by the imaginations of any or if possible by the doing of those innocent thoughts.

Do you not see Gabriel that thoughts and imaginations are not plans and schemes? This is of no offense to Elohim and certainly of no threat; for he knows who he is. And I my brother know who I am and who I am not. But for freedom's sake, I allow for no barriers and hindrances in my imaginations. To do so would be truly an offence to the one who made me."

As clear and precise as Lucifer's argument seemed, Gabriel struggled to come to a place of accord. It became clear to Gabriel that this was Heaven's first debate and surely the end of it must be unity.

"Lucifer;" challenged Gabriel. "It seems to me that your freedom must be held in the firm hands of your will; and your will must be wholly submitted to your King and his purposes. Do your imaginations rule your will or does your will rule your imaginations?

You say you are free to imagine for there is no harm if your will cannot make it true. But I say you are free to NOT imagine and to choose NOT to dwell on what is of no benefit or profit. Lucifer, hold tight your freedom. Rule over it and do not let it rule you."

Lucifer was quick to respond; "What you call freedom is more than bondage to me and to all who would know true freedom."

"Then in a good and pleasant bondage we are. Never should we want freedom from it," declared Gabriel.

Lucifer smirked and almost scoffing said; "You speak of bondage to one who fulfills his destiny in freedom. In this we are parted or lack understanding."

Lucifer challenged Gabriel, "Am I not free?"

Gabriel answered "Free he has made you; free to love and sing and play and work; to think and create."

As Gabriel continued to look at the beautiful creature before him, something changed, shifted. So small was this change, it was almost imperceptible. In the smallest possible portion of time, there was what seemed to Gabriel a flash in Lucifer's appearance, though the very opposite of a flash of light. It was almost as if the light of Elohim that burned bright in Lucifer subsided or was in some way diminished. Gabriel's disposition changed as well and was equally as subtle so that Lucifer who was busy with his own thoughts could not quite see it. But within Gabriel was something more severe than he had ever known. Something had changed.

Lucifer's question, Gabriel thought, seemed intended not to seek an answer but to make his own point.

Lucifer asked; "But am I free in all of this only to serve? Is my gift to Elohim my own, from my own heart by my own will? Am I free only to serve and give? If free then am I not also free to be more than a giver of gifts and a servant? Am I not free to be more than this? Am I not free to be all I desire to be? Where is my freedom if I am only a gift and a giver of gifts and only the servant of another? Is my music my own or only his? And what of my art and the creations of my hands? Are they not mine as well as his?"

Gabriel did not respond to the questions as he knew full well that Lucifer already had confidence in his own answers.

Lucifer continued, "I am a gift, truly. All I do and all my art is a gift from him and for him. And though I am happy to be so and do so, is this the sum of my being? Am I only a gift bearer? If this is true, where then is my freedom?"

Gabriel sensed that this discussion was unlike any other they had ever had and was immensely critical. He felt there was a cloud of misunderstanding, something never before known in Heaven. And although something in him wished he were elsewhere, he felt as if he needed to stand and be heard. And in continued trust of his brother and friend, he did not answer Lucifer's questions. But in his mind Gabriel stood to the side, out of the path of Lucifer's words and was determined not to hear Lucifer further until Lucifer would hear him. And with measured tone and strength of expression, Gabriel tried to pull Lucifer out of a cloud of twisted reason into clarity.

"Your words have failed you;" pronounced Gabriel with a confidence easily seen by Lucifer. "Your intentions are betrayed by a debate that ill represents your true nature. For I know and trust that your intentions are not well expressed in this discourse. For though you are Heaven's great craftsman, who paints and sculpts with tongue and speech, words have failed you and failed us both.

We have strayed off the path of clarity and purpose. I know that one so wise as you could not be so blind as this dialogue would suggest. I think not. It is not the craftsman who has failed here, but the tools in his able hands. Surely, this is only speech that poorly reflects your true heart. And now, I desire only to remind you of what you must surely see and understand. For it cannot be otherwise my good friend."

Gabriel once again drew close to Lucifer and this time it was he who spoke as if to a student.

"Surely;" he petitioned with the gentlest of voice, "you know that freedom is nothing if it does not birth love and life. And you know my brother that the gift of music, of art and of poetry that you offer to Elohim is as well his gift to you. For you and you alone stand in his majesty with no restraint. Though we all see him, you are given the privilege of bringing constant joy to his heart. And is not his laughter and joy enough for you? Does his appreciation and thankful heart not fill you to the brim? You and you alone are given the keys of music and beauty that knows no equal being only surpassed by the sound of his voice and his song, of which you daily partake. Your gift to Elohim is his gift to you. None could be more happy.

Free he has indeed made you. But freedom without restraint is unthinkable folly."

Lucifer responded. "And thankful I will always be that he made me to create and give. I could never take what I desire at his expense. Is it so wrong to create my hearts desire and take pleasure for myself and to give a gift to myself while never ceasing to offer to him what he rightly deserves? I am free indeed. This I know more than you. But if your words be true, then my freedom is held in closed fists for purposes other than mine.

Is freedom only a word to you?"

Gabriel abandoned his gentle speech and drew back a few steps from Lucifer. With sterner words, he once more warned his friend. "Be careful my brother and friend for if your thoughts stray but a little to the left or right you shall live your days in sorrow."

Lucifer felt the intended bite of Gabriel's words and was provoked to even harder words.

"You would my friend restrain my thoughts and my imagination," said Lucifer with raised voice. "For without imagination, there can be no creativity, no music, no beauty and no gift.

Your words Gabriel are equally false as I know you would not dare to hinder what Elohim has created in me. My days are not for you to measure and my end is not in your hands. I know that my freedom will stretch your mind, for your own purposes need no such creativity. But take this warning well Gabriel; judge not my own design and purpose.

It is my nature to imagine and there is no wrong in that. I know you do not intend, my brother, to suggest err where there is none. Only Elohim can recall what he has birthed in my heart. I am what he desires, and freedom and imagination is the field into which the seeds of creativity are planted. I know that no one as high and perfect as you could wrongly judge this true servant of the most high Elohim.

And so you have rightly said, it is but words that hinder your true acceptance of my good intentions. Though you may not see it, I am free to think and to act and to hope and desire without restraint.

I am happy to be what he has made me to be. Still my artist mind wonders of what is not; but perhaps could be. And so hear my question once again and answer me truly for I know not yet your heart in these simple things. Answer this I pray; am I not free to wonder?"

Gabriel once again stepped back into the conversation, but unrest was deep in his heart though he did not know what it was.

Slowly he answered. "Wonder yes; desire no. For all your desire should be his desire. This is the best and highest. In that place and no other, there is life and peace and joy."

Lucifer felt Gabriel soften and continued; "Am I not standing in his light, Gabriel? Are my thoughts not like shouted words to him? I am not in secret hiding am I? For all my heart and mind is known to him. The words I speak to you, he hears and knows and I too know of his hearing.

So how can I stray when all is open and all is in constant light? I speak in the light. I think in the light. Is this not the humility in which Elohim delights; to think freely and speak freely knowing that none can escape him?"

Gabriel's unease continued and for the first time he felt trapped in this debate that held no joy for him, and though he longed for it to end, Gabriel could see no escape. Difficult as it was, his heart was still for Lucifer. For until now, he had always marveled at Lucifer's deep thoughts and wisdom. Still in Gabriel's unease, there was no offence, only trust and hope that all of this would end well.

"My friend;" said Gabriel, "one cannot hide where there is no hiding place and yet it is nonetheless… "

Gabriel hesitated and for the first time ever was lost for words. His heart looked for that which he could not find.

Now there was in the language of angels no word for "evil" or "wrong" or "wicked" for the speech of man and the birth of malice was yet far off.

Gabriel found the word and continued; "regrettable" he repeated. "One cannot hide where there is no hiding place and yet it is nonetheless regrettable if hiding is the heart's pleasure. The lack of opportunity is in no way humility."

Lucifer continued with words no less forceful, "You impugn me my brother. And I fear it is because I think more freely than you. This freedom is not of my own will. For my will is the fruit of Elohim's will. If he created me to be free and think and to create, would it not be foolish for me to deny my freedom? My freedom is created by him for his delight. There can be no song, no gift to him without this freedom."

Gabriel responded, "Your words are sweet. They tax the mind and pull at the heart, and that is the fruit of your freedom. For I swear Lucifer, your greatest craft is in your words. And what a masterpiece you have fashioned this day with your words, your sweet words.

But hear me, your freedom is better spent creating for Elohim rather than conjuring for yourself and contesting with your brother and friend."

Lucifer could see the weight on Gabriel brought on by this conversation. There was until that moment a certain joy in the wooing of Gabriel to Lucifer's position. It felt to him a challenge to debate and win Gabriel's mind in these matters. But now he stood before Gabriel wondering if something was broken that moments before was whole. What Lucifer thought was innocent debate, now seemed to threaten unity and friendship. This was not Lucifer's cause or aim.

In softer tone, Lucifer continued, "Forgive me my brother if ever you thought that I would control your mind with words to my own benefit. Am I not his servant and your friend? Am I not an Archangel as are you? Do I not command the thousands entrusted to me as do you? Am I not in authority over many and trusted with a host of his servants as are you?

I will ever love you for we are the same brethren and equals. And I trust you will ever give me your heart and allegiance. I now humble myself before you for any offence my freedom has caused."

Gabriel sensed something stirring in him from the Spirit of Elohim; as if Elohim had reached out a finger to touch him and bid him to speak on his behalf.

"Lucifer;" said Gabriel with a strength that made Lucifer lift his head, "I speak to you now as Gabriel the servant of the most high. And my words are not mine alone. Take heed and warning; for there is a shadow over you of your own creation. As yet it has no substance, but a hair's breath separates you from a destiny that is not of Elohim.

If I loved you not, I could give no such challenge. You are the anointed one, chosen by him. Your beauty is unsurpassed. When you walk the paths of Heaven, all look in awe. But though every heart is smitten by such beauty, all give honor to Elohim who made you and entrusted you with such high purposes. You would do well to do the same.

Guard your heart. For there is a door set before you beyond which is a crooked path and your hand is nesting on the handle of that door."

Quietly Lucifer responded; "If I have caused your heart to worry let me now assure you of my friendship to you and my devotion to the "Being one." I will forever be his servant and son. I cannot but serve Elohim and bring joy to him that only I can bring. And you shall continue to witness in Lucifer; the Shining One, a life surrendered to Elohim."

Now Lucifer rose up and once more as if to correct a wayward child, spoke with more than equal strength. "Now let me warn you as well of the path of judgment that you may well choose this day. It is not a path of friendship. Be wary of what door your hand rests upon."

Lucifer's voice lowered and he looked into the eyes of Gabriel. In consoling words intended to bring unneeded assurance, he continued.

"And think not, my brother, of any false judgment in your heart. For I know your true desires. It shall not be counted against you by either me or Elohim. You are his true servant and my true friend. We shall not talk of offence for I am not wronged. It is but words, vapor that cannot diminish my love for you. And be at peace Gabriel, for I am certain Elohim finds no offence in rash words. Though harsh, they remain innocent. And you could only ever be innocent. You are blessed and his love overlooks all things."

Gabriel departed, but for the first time the ease and peace of Heaven felt frail and fragile. Gabriel flew toward the Citadel leaving Lucifer there in the tower above the garden. As he flew, he pondered the words of Lucifer. There was a feeling in his heart he had never known. He slowed his flight and did not want to stand in the King's Court with such a heavy heart. For a long while, he challenged this feeling and wondered what this foreign invader in his heart meant. Where did it come from? And where would it lead?

5

The Rival Prince

Gabriel entered the Citadel where Michael rose to meet him before the throne of Elohim. Together, they approached the light until they became light, translucent reflections awash in the aura of the great "I am."

And there in the throne room of Elohim, all angelic beings had parted being dismissed by Elohim for a time. This was rare but on occasion served the purposes of Elohim. Michael and Gabriel were not amazed to find such silence and quiet in this place of celebration.

Elohim spoke; "What is this I see in your heart Gabriel? What thought has birthed this disquiet in you?"

"I know not, my King," said Gabriel, "but it grows and rules over other thoughts and feelings. It is nothing I have known and no words can tell. But you my Lord surely know. And so now I ask you, Father what is this thing?"
"Where have you been?" asked Elohim.

"Lord you know I have been with your servant Lucifer. And there, while in discourse with him, this intruder in my heart crept through some unguarded gate. Tell me Lord what is this?"

"The peace that you have always known has been challenged my son," said Elohim.

"Strong and unshakable, this peace is here in this place and always in my presence, but your spirit senses a threat to all peace. As of now, this threat is groundless, a fantasy. But in your heart an unseen and unknown danger lurks.

Your heart knows only peace and never have you known anything but the joy of Heaven. But now, deep in the quiet of your thoughts, there is that which might come to pass. It has no name and no substance. It is but a possibility that stirs and provokes your peace. You sense what might be. Your mind foresees what your eyes and your heart have no knowledge of."

"But Lord," said Gabriel. "How can these things be? Lucifer is as I am and all that he is comes from you. This unease can only be my own folly. Forgive me Lord for this disturbance. Surely, it comes from somewhere in my heart without reason or purpose or even hearts desire.

Why did his words score me so? And even as I listened to him, my heart burned. And in my heart, I stood against him and his strange imaginations. Lord, I spoke a warning to him as if from you. But perhaps it was my own zeal. Do I stand in need of correction?"

"You need no correction Gabriel my son," spoke Elohim, "for you did indeed speak my words before your brother. You sensed my heart and stood in my stead. Your feelings are with good cause and yet they are not of what is, but what could be. Though it is unthinkable, Lucifer is standing at the edge of Heaven, of life and of love looking out beyond their walls."

"Lord, I know my brother through and through and yet never as you do. What device does he possess that you have not birthed in him for your own purposes? And can it be my Lord that what you have given him can in any way come to ruin? What, my King, in this is your will and your purpose?"

Gabriel glanced around and then shook his head in disbelief, confused and puzzled. He continued to question.

"Should I know such unrest in my heart for what might come to be? Come or not come, is it not from you? Can anything escape your will?"

"My will, Gabriel", said Elohim "is not a prison or cage from which any should escape or run. My will, as yours, serves a greater master; my love. And in my love and devotion there is no captivity from which to run. For my will serves my love and my love seeks only the best and highest for all in my realm. To escape my will, as you put it, is truly to run from my love. You and all your brethren are fashioned by love and for love. There is no escaping where there are no closed doors, no locks, no keys, no bonds or grasping hands.

Should a creature of the sea wish to escape the very water that brings him life? Should a bird of the air wish to escape the sky? Such is my love and such is my will."

"Father, I know well that there is only love in your heart. How than can one formed by your hand be less than that love and less than your will? In all I see and have known, there is no place to move and think and imagine beyond your love and will. I seem unable to understand Lucifer's imaginations. And I cannot grasp his purpose or your will in what he imagines."

"And what of your imaginations Gabriel?" said Elohim. "Do you think that I command the heart to imagine what I will? In this, both you and Lucifer have some understanding but neither has the whole. He looks to freedom and sees no rule or command there. And so he freely imagines. This is true in part.

You look to love and see only agreeable submission. But you too imagine just as freely as he.

Understand this my son; freedom and submission are not in conflict. For freedom to dream must be tempered with love and obligation. One can imagine as one will and in the end there is little more than a dream. The mind can imagine a path without ever walking down that path - this is innocence.

But dreaming can indeed lead to the very opposite of innocence when love and honor submit to freedom; when freedom reigns. Freedom should always serve the heart, submit to love and give way to those whom you love.

But when freedom becomes the head and love the tail, dreams and desires can reach beyond the confines of love and obligation."

Gabriel stood quietly trying to grasp these words.

Elohim continued, "I have given a gift of which I will not repent. In this, Lucifer is right. He and you as well are free to imagine. But love must govern all.

There is another road unseen, a path that resides only in Lucifer's mind. For you it is a fearful thing. For Lucifer it is idle rambling of little consequence.

What Lucifer imagines has no opportunity and can never be. He is free to wonder what it is to be as I am. But that which his mind proposes could never be anything more than wonder.

What you imagine however can indeed come to pass.

And in this I have not steered either you or your brother."

"But Lord," Gabriel asked. "Why should Lucifer dream of what is not and can never be? And if only a dream then all is well, is it not? For what evil can come from impossible dreams?"

"It is not in dreaming and it is not in the doing of what cannot be done;" responded Elohim. "Dreaming is the nature and heart of Lucifer's gift. For his music and art and beauty must begin as a dream. And when he puts desire to that dream, the dream is fueled and comes to life. And when he puts his will to desire, it becomes substantial and takes form for all hearts to hold and all eyes to see and all ears to hear. He is the builder of dreams for the joy of all. But his thoughts of late have no such potential to be. They are aimless dreams. They go nowhere and accomplish nothing. For now, he dreams to dream and imagines what may be without foul intent.

But these dreams can give birth to a dark and fearful thing. Two things are but lacking. For then and only then can this darkness be made whole and potent.

If Lucifer adds to his imagination strong desire, it will be folly, for he can never be more than he is given to be. And if he adds to his desire the will and determination to make it so, then and only then will his destiny be altered. His dreams can never be, but his heart can desire that which is unprofitable and his will can create a crooked path, one that is never in my heart or will for any.

Your heart is troubled for you know he may and can choose that dark path."

"Then is Lucifer in error? And can we not appeal to his love and his wisdom?" asked Gabriel.

"He is now leaning toward error but as yet, there is no error for true freedom is his," said Elohim. "And there is still an innocence in the core of his heart. I would that love be his goal for everything he dreams. Still, his love, as his imaginations, are his own. For love is not love unless freely given.

Though he has to this hour given me his love freely, it is his to give and the hour next it will continue to be so.

To his wisdom, I have already appealed through your own converse. For in your speaking was my heart and will.

But what is wisdom?

Like you, what Lucifer values, he loves, and what he loves, he desires. That which he desires he freely chooses. And by his will he moves to do and act accordingly. All that is before him here in Heaven is a treasure to rightly value always. Should he fail to value these great treasures, then he may also fail in the loving and the choosing. Then and only then shall wisdom descend into madness."

"Father," said Gabriel "forgive my lack of understanding. But how could any that come from your bosom fail to value what should be valued; fail to love what should be loved? Surely, this can never happen. How can one not see what is simply there to see? When their eyes meet what is before them, when they look to you and all that is in your heart, all that you have done; surely, they cannot fail to see and value and love and choose as they should."

Elohim answered once again. "In this, my son, is a mystery which I share with you and Michael alone. For your love and innocence are perfected and can no longer be tried. Those to whom I have given the gift of freedom can see what the heart desires to see though it be fancy and folly. This is a deep mystery but I will open the eyes of your heart.

If error there be, and error beyond measure, it is in calling darkness light and light darkness. It is seeing as if real that which is not real. It is in loving that which has no value. It is possible for one to see what he desires to see - what he wants to see. And in the seeing of what is not, become blind to what is. This is deception of which Heaven has no knowledge. It is difficult for you to understand because deception is foreign to all.

But because of freedom and imagination, hearts can see what hearts will. And that which is false can seem as if real and that which is true appears to the heart as false. This is true blindness and a deep darkness that resists the light of truth. All fails when speculation becomes real in the heart. When deception is birthed, it has the power to resist even the will and revelation of Elohim.

This is insanity for which there is little remedy. And if there is a cure and healing for such deception, it begins in the heart with a desire to know what is and to forsake what is not. If hearts ever venture down the dark and terrible path of deception, only a genuine hunger for truth can lead them home again."

Tears welled up in Gabriel's bright eyes. "Will this happen to my brother and friend whom I dearly love?" asked Gabriel.

Elohim stepped forward and in the form of his choosing emerged out of the white light that encompassed the throne. His face was not hidden from Gabriel or Michael and his eyes spoke as much as his words.

"His destiny is in his seeing and choosing," said Elohim. "It is not known what he will choose to see. But while there is love and joy in this realm of mine, there is a strong hand to guide him and steer his course to safer shores. Love is not finished with him and it is unthinkable that he should ever be finished with love. Still, it is not easy to stop a falling pillar, especially when the pillar is determined to fall."

Michael who was all this time kneeling before the throne rose before Elohim and stood beside Gabriel.

"Father, what shall we do?" asked Michael.

Elohim drew back into the light upon the throne and was again swallowed by the light that grew even brighter. From the throne, there rang such a sound strong and sweet to the ears and heart. All of Gabriel's disquiet and unrest vanished in the presence of Elohim.

"I am" sang Elohim. "I am," came an echoing concert from the throne; "I am."

As all of Heaven heaved and swayed at the song of Elohim, joy deeper than Gabriel had ever known flowed through him. The strength and courage of the King surged through him and his heart was settled.

All the while, Michael was at Gabriel's side standing erect and tall before the throne. Gabriel turned to Michael and for the first time saw there a warrior of awesome strength and courage. And never in

Heaven was there need for such strength and might before. And though brothers and friends for ages past, Gabriel had taken little notice of Michael's stature and unyielding form. Imposing and regal was he in the light of Elohim.

Gabriel spoke to Michael, "I am mindful of your might and vigilance my brother and I have always known its source but never imagined its need. And now I see, though the foundations of Heaven crumble, nothing shall hinder the purposes of Elohim. For Father, Son and Spirit are all and in all. He is the great "I am" and none shall shake him as he is not unawares. This you have always known Michael, for in you is his might; Oh guardian of Heaven, and none shall shake you. For in your being is a breath of his strength and it is enough to accomplish all that his heart intends."

Gabriel grasped Michael's arm and declared, "Oh mighty warrior!"

Michael smiled and spoke, " I, brother, long for your heart. You have all wisdom and speak for Elohim. You are his heart and voice. You are the trusted one. My strength will forever serve you as it does my King."

The Archangels embraced before Elohim's throne and an alliance of strength and wisdom and compassion was made that very hour.

Now Elohim summoned all of Heaven before him and Michael stood at his right side and Gabriel stood at his left. Lucifer drew close to the throne and raised his hands before Elohim. A mighty host of angels rose to the heights of the great hall and began a symphony as Lucifer sang a verse of worship before the King.

>	The three in one and one in three and love of all to all
>	A majesty beyond all else, the King of Heaven's hall
>
>	Where gold and crystal, light and song proclaim the worthy one
>	And all bow low before the Father, the Spirit and the Son.
>
>	Where Spirit moves upon the lake and trees sing loud his praise
>	And Heaven's host declare his worth, in song through endless days
>
>	Here too stand Lucifer before the throne in majesty and light
>	Formed and fashioned by his hand, perfect in beauty and in might
>
>	And through the greatness found therein, his greatness is declared
>	Who forged such beauty found in me that none in Heaven share.

In the midst of the noise and movement and celebration, there seemed a shrill tone struck in the music in discord with all else. Though not every ear could hear, both Michael and Gabriel took notice and stood silent. For never was there in the music of Heaven any sound or note that did not blend and add to the harmony; whether it be Elohim or

Lucifer or the singing of angels or the music that rose from the crystal waters of Heaven. And for a moment, there seemed something amiss in Heaven, something out of concert, out of key.

Elohim drew forth out of the light that was all around the throne and his form could be seen by all. Elohim raised his hands and all motion stopped, all music ceased and not a sound was heard. The deepest silence all creation had ever known was everywhere and nothing stirred.

Elohim looked to Lucifer whose hands were still raised but he too was silent and still.

"Lucifer," spoke Elohim in a gentle tone. "What fills your mind and heart that you would sing and play so? And why do you present a song to me that so thinly disguises your true thoughts and ambitions? For you have chosen this day to sing of your greatness and present it to all. What lurks in your heart and mind to bring such disharmony."

"My Lord," said Lucifer, "it is too much for me to see your displeasure. I am bowed low to the breaking of my heart."

"Lucifer," said Elohim still with gentle voice; "you have yet to know my displeasure and you shall surely taste first of my mercy."

"Mercy my Lord?" Lucifer looked truly perplexed. "And for what should I desire this? What fault lies within me that I should appeal for mercy?"

Elohim continued "My child whom I have created with my own hand and have loved as well as all and more; do you think so highly of yourself as to forget the source of your life and value and cause? Why should you proclaim your worth more loudly than all else?"

Lucifer fell to his knees before the throne and in but a whisper replied, "My King, I desire only that all who know me and see me and witness the wonder that I am, give homage to my maker and my King, who is the rightful heir to all glory and honor bestowed on me. I am but a vessel who receives and returns all to you. The admiration I bestow upon myself is multiplied in the tribute extended to you. And once I part with the honor, I swear there is none left for me. It is all laid at your feet for your glory alone."

"My son, hear my words" said Elohim. "It is enough to know your worth and rest in the knowledge of your great value and import, but there is no profit to encourage it so greatly from others or to shrewdly seek it in rivalry."

"Rivalry my Lord?" puzzled Lucifer. "I do not know the concept. Your wisdom and sight are beyond mine and you must see in me what is hidden from me. Who Lord is my rival in this place called Heaven where all is free and all is safe and all is loved and all is honored? I am in your bosom, rested and secure, and feel no threat of diminishing; and am confident I shall never lack worth, whether in my own eyes or the eyes of others. Who then is my rival? For I greatly honor Michael and Gabriel who are very close to me in worth and value. Shed your light my Lord on my darkness if there be any. Who is my rival?"

Elohim answered, "You have made me your rival. You, my son, contend and compete for that which I am and have, though you are already full to the brim. There is no more room in you for greater. You have partaken of all I can give you. And here is your blindness that you would desire and seek even more."

Lucifer had no response but hung his head in silence and searched his heart and mind for he knew that Elohim had perfect sight.

"Lucifer," Elohim continued; "Do you think I would rob you of your honor?"

Lucifer with head lowered answered the question with less strength in his mighty voice than Heaven knew.

"You cannot steal that which you rightly own," he said. "You have all honor and have shared it with all, but it is yours, not for me to give, but for you to take at will."

"Lucifer," asked Elohim again, "do you believe I would ever rob you of your honor?"

"Is it mine to have? I think not my Lord. For I am but a steward of honor bestowed on me. You shall take it from my hands at your own counsel and not of my will or desire. It is always yours though it rests great on me."

"Lucifer," asked Elohim, "do you believe I would rob you of your honor?"

Lucifer realized that Elohim's question was not about honor but of the heart and motive of Elohim. Lucifer hung a heavy head and no angelic being had ever frowned so until now.

"No my Lord, it is not within you. You should never take what you have given. You would never rob me of my honor or any such thing," sighed Lucifer.

With strong and louder but still gentle voice, Elohim said "Then why my son of sons, who shines for all and is perfect and complete, whom I love and have denied nothing, why do you seek to rob me of mine?"

"Lord have I done so? Can I do that which I would loathe above all things? Could I ever rob you of your glory? And if I have taken glory belonging to you, how can I return what is rightfully yours?" cried Lucifer.

Elohim answered in a voice that no one had ever heard with an expression never before seen or imagined on the face of Elohim. In sorrow that could be seen by all eyes and felt by every heart in Heaven.

"No, Lucifer," spoke Elohim, "it is not within your power or craft or in any to take from me unless it is given. But though you cannot, it is in your heart to try and in this is my heart wounded. For you desire to have what is not yours to have, to be what is not yours to be, to take what is not yours to take. You have dreamed dreams of being and doing but you fail to see that your being can reach no higher and your deeds will never be greater and your art and music can excel no more in my eyes. Your gift to me has always been precious. And until this day, your song has been the song in my heart declaring to all my love. It has always been a treasure for all in Heaven. It is not your gift but your heart that makes it so. And now your gift is pale as your heart has wandered from its light and life.

Lucifer, you cannot be as I am and never should you desire such. And now you have brought to Heaven that which is not in my heart. Born in you is a false hunger that can never be satisfied. Oh, to desire what you can never have, to try to take what can not be taken - this is grief for all.

Now, you have but one recourse. And this must be your great desire now. It is for you to bring to end all your contemplations, speculations and desires. This door you have opened must be shut and locked, the key discarded to never be opened again"

Now Heaven had never known sadness until this very hour. It began in the heart of Elohim and continued in Lucifer. This day tears were shed not of joy as all Heaven knew, but of weary heart that saw what no heart should ever see; that which was loved and trusted and lost. For there in Heaven that day trust was broken; a grave error of judgment made. It was the first foul step on a new and dark path that never was in the heart of Elohim. And it was the first moment when wisdom failed, and the very first time mercy on the heels of sorrow was offered.

Elohim wept and Lucifer wept and all Heaven wept.

Lucifer lifted his head ever so slightly to see all of Heaven looking to him. He cried out "Lord this is too much to bear. How can these things be in me? How can I purge myself of this arrogance. And Lord how can I ever win your heart and trust again. Help me Lord for I cannot bear to see a tear shed by such as you, the creator and Father of all. There is a heavy burden on me, a shadow of guilt that breaks my spirit, a judgment too grave for me. What shall I do? Should I ever know joy again?"

Lucifer's heart was truly broken and the severity of his thoughts and imaginations were now revealed. For in that very hour, he had desired what he had only imagined and in irreverent song proclaimed it. Elohim reached out his hand and lifted Lucifer to his feet. Lucifer could not look into the eyes of Elohim.

Elohim spoke; "My son, now you know my displeasure and you have marked it well. You have joined with me in grief for that which is in your heart. And now in sorrow and repentance you have changed your mind again and regained the path that I intended for you. So you shall know my mercy. And because you have measured your error and your pride and found it reckless as it is, you are forgiven and healed.

But Lucifer, you are still the master of your thoughts and desires; and you must learn from this lapse of sanity. You must deny yourself the privilege of dreams for a time until all is surrendered without doubt, and trust is won again. For though I love you dearly, you have broken something that in time and service will mend."

"Lord," sobbed Lucifer, "I am broken and will devote myself to my correction. For all my gifts and arts shall be for you and none for me. The songs that I sing shall even more elevate your goodness; for your love is shown in mercy today for one who deserves neither."

"And in this, I am pleased" said Elohim. "But Lucifer, know this that your gift has always been your own. But your heart and devotion has been mine until this day. This is a lesson worth learning and learn it you will, but not in your high service to me. You shall stand down from your duty and your post to serve another for a time. You shall call Michael your Lord and serve him with all your heart until all is restored and all is mended. In this, you will find healing and understanding. Humility shall be your reward and nonetheless shall you fully know true worth and value in due time. So let your repentance become soft and serving of another for your great good and the benefit of all."

Lucifer felt all eyes on him as he stood before the throne. The weight of Elohim's judgment was equal to the guilt that was lifted from him. And he stretched out his hand for the mercy of Elohim, but suffered to love his rebuke. Still, did he abide by the words and judgments administered that hour. But strong was his desire to be fully restored to his post and honor in the presence of Elohim.

And for a time, he was made a Captain to Michael and served him well. And he looked the part of a humble servant, but in his heart was unrest. No words he spoke would ever reflect the impatience growing in his heart. Each day, he was sure would be the day of his reinstatement, and each day it was held from him and each day he knew displeasure greater than the day before. Still, he served and was quiet in his discontent. And daily, he trained his thoughts and barred his mind until there were in him no misdirected imaginations. In his mind, he became pure again, but in his heart was some undefined agitation.

6

The New Realm

Now, there were no days in Heaven, as man would know days, marked by the rising or setting of sun, but days there were. And each day, every hour and portion was known better by angels than might ever be measured by any device yet to come in the world of man. There were times for work and rest and times for play. There were times for quiet and stillness and times for rousing, for song and dance. There were times for building and growing. There were high times of celebration and low times of meditation. And there were times when light burned brightly and times where dimmer was the light in Heaven. Never was there sleep for all beings of angel kind knew no weariness or fatigue. Still there were times of softness and quietness and times for refreshing.

And when that day came, no heralds were required, no announcements made, no call of assembly was ushered from the Citadel of Elohim. From the far reaches of Heaven creatures stirred and moved and all were drawn to the great hall though none had called. For all of Heaven could feel in their hearts that Elohim was ready. Why this day and not the one before or after would never be known as only Elohim understood the times and seasons of his plans and purposes.

As the throngs drew toward the fire of Elohim that rose even beyond the roof of Heaven, whispers could be heard from one end of Heaven to the other; "It is time." The murmur rose to a thunderous din like a great falling of waters into deep pools. "It is time." "It is time," echoed off the jeweled walls and tumbled down the golden paths skipping across the crystal waters. "It is time." Then a great hush came upon those who entered the Citadel. The first to come were Michael with Lucifer at his side and Gabriel close behind. Michael and Gabriel in reverence and excitement made their way to their place at the right and left of Elohim. All of Heaven poured into the arena and silence swept over all.

Lucifer heard only to himself the call of Elohim to take his place before the throne and to take up his command once again of the great host appointed to him. And never was there more pleasure in an angel heart when he did so. But as he did, he knew all eyes were on Elohim and few would notice his reinstatement. Though none would know except Elohim himself, Lucifer's heart sank just a little at the lack ceremony and pageantry that surely befit a circumstance such as this. For long he had waited and much he endured to regain what he had lost. And his accomplishment would be lost in the greater purpose of this gathering.

Lucifer stood silently before the throne. And all were transfixed. Michael and Gabriel were set to burst for excitement.

Elohim in concert, Father, Son and Spirit, spoke out; "Let there be." His words became substantial and flowed through the hall of halls and over the Crystal Lake. And Elohim raised his hands. A thunderous sound rose from the Crystal Sea. Shimmering water from the midst of the Crystal Sea rose up to meet him in a pillar of sparkling light. All of Heaven's host moved back away from the water to the outer walls of the great hall and to the shores beyond the far side of the sea. The sea became alive swaying and rocking and rising to the command of the King. The water rose from the great Lake into the sky of Heaven forming a pillar suspended above the sea. The glass-like surface of the sea around the pillar still shimmered and reflected a mirror image of the Citadel. Its waters gently heaved and rolled now stirred by the rising pillar above the Lake. A darker, wavering reflection of the pillar could be seen by all on the surface of the water – a pillar above, and a dark shadow and reflection of the same below. The dark reflection became deeper and more vivid; more than light bouncing off the surface of the water. This was no mere reflection. It had shape and dimension, depth and breadth. It was in truth an inverted pillar like the one above of equal size and girth. This column stretched down, through and below the surface - mirroring the pillar above the sea. And in the midst of the sea, that which at first seemed only a reflection appeared now as a shadowy shaft of water lesser and distant and dark.

This shaft of lesser water began to spread downward and outward growing and thinning as it grew. The column expanded outward in length and width diminishing in light until its edges moved beyond sight. It was no longer a shaft and no longer the image of the bright water of Heaven. Now through the surface of the Crystal Sea like a lens, another world could be seen as born in the heart of Heaven - not so much a different world as a different realm touching Heaven - together and yet apart. The sea of Heaven became like a lens through which one could see the endless space of this lesser world. It was not a world of light but of darkness. This darkness, no angel eye had ever seen. And like the endless soft white space and sky that surrounded Heaven, another space could be seen through the mirror of the Lake but dark it was, untouched by the light of Heaven. And two worlds existed, one on top of the other; not separate but not together. Like threads within a tapestry, these worlds were woven together - one side, the light of Heaven; the other, the darkness of a new creation. And as all eyes looked to the Lake, a dark empty eternity stood before all.

Now the water of light that Elohim had called forth from the Crystal Lake stood as a pillar above the Lake. And on the other side of the Lake was a new world. And Elohim raised his hands. A single drop of water fell not into the Lake but through the Lake into the world of darkness. It grew in size and diminished in light as it pierced the darkness. Now this wobbling orb of water from Heaven floated in endless space; empty and void. It turned and moved and yet held together trembling and quivering and growing ever larger until it became a massive sphere of water in this world without light. And the Spirit of Elohim flowed from the throne as a whisper of light, a glowing mist sinking into the Lake and beyond to the new world below. The

Spirit surrounded the water and flowed over the great dark and empty void.

Elohim spoke to the water as the Spirit hovered over it and said; "Let there be light." And where the Spirit moved across the great sphere that hung in the space of this new world, there was light, but not as the light of Heaven. Pale was this light and made of a slighter substance. This was a light made for lesser eyes to see. Still light it was, but far removed from light that was known in Heaven whose source was Elohim.

And the pleasure of Elohim was everywhere as the light was good in his eyes.

And there was now both light and darkness. And the darkness came down on one side of the great, empty sphere while light shone down the other side.

Then Elohim spoke and said, "So shall man measure his life in days of light and dark. The light shall be for his sight and his endeavors and the shade of night shall be for his rest and his comfort. This shall be his day and mark his journey in numbers through time."

And angels watched as the first day and night of this new world unfolded and came to an end.

In the turning of the great sphere, the second day of light shone through and around the waters. And Elohim spoke the words, "Let there be" and the sphere of water shook and trembled and divided, not from left to right or top to bottom but from inner to outer. The core of the great sphere remained while the surface of the sphere lifted and separated above the core and in between was space and a sky dividing the sphere and the outer skin of the world. There was water surrounded by empty space surrounded again by water and mist. And the sky between the waters amplified the light and the darkness and colours flowed in and through the sky. And above the sky was a thin canopy of water like a shining, shimmering tent above the world.

And Elohim's pleasure was known by all as this new world's second day was complete.

Elohim spoke yet again as the Spirit continued to hover over the great and empty waters; "Let there be." Out of the waters of the sphere came a fabric more firm and rigid than the water that birthed it. It was rock and stone and earth and sand and gem and jewel and metal. And this land formed as a crust around the sphere of water and the Earth was born. Now the waters were in the midst of the Earth but flowed into huge seas and lakes scattered around the Earth. And surface of the land took shape and there were valleys and hills and mountains, streams and lakes and the great seas. And the light shone no longer through the sphere but fell down one side as darkness fell against the other.

Then Elohim said, "Let there be" and as the Spirit hovered there around the Earth, life came to the land. Growing, living things began to rise up toward Heaven. Small invisible life moved and grew within the soil and waters. Grass and plant, tree and flower, vine and bush spread across the globe digging deep into the soil and reaching up toward the sky. Fruit and flower were everywhere and seeds fell and spores took flight and everywhere was life.

And so ended the third day of the new creation. And through the Crystal Lake, all of Heaven could see in the dim twilight a world of wonder full of life and growing things. This world was a garden. Unlike the gardens of Heaven, they were fragile indeed, but a marvel to look upon. And still the pleasure of all that was complete that day filled Elohim's heart.

Lucifer, amazed at this growing world of frail beauty, both loved what his eyes beheld but puzzled at the delight in which Elohim's heart abounded. For though it was indeed grand, it was not as Heaven was. He could see this new world as little more than clay in need of a sculptor or canvas in need of an artist. Lucifer turned to Gabriel in a quiet moment as all eyes were on this new world and asked "Why does Elohim marvel so when equal beauty less frail and more substantial is all around him in this Heaven that we know?"

Gabriel not wanting to be drawn from his attention to all Elohim was doing answered abruptly. "It is not what he has created alone that brings him such joy and to which his heart is pleased. It is for whom he has prepared these things. For all is a gift for the coming ones and Elohim declares that it is a good and acceptable gift for ones so dear and precious to his heart."

Lucifer could see Gabriel was less interested in conversation and so fell silent again.

Elohim spoke again the words of creation "Let there be."

And on this fourth day in the new world, the work of Elohim continued to the marvel of silent spectators. With raised hands, Elohim called forth the pillar of water that still hung above the Crystal Sea of Heaven. At the sound of his voice, the waters obeyed their Lord and with an explosive, almost violent assault plunged into and through the Lake to the new world. With a deafening blast and a brilliant blaze of light, the waters shattered into countless drops. So bright and loud was the spectacle that hardly a head could keep from turning away, too bright for even angel eyes. The countless pearls of water became white hot spores of light in the new world. They scattered at the speed of Elohim's thoughts throughout the space of the new creation. And these shining shards of crystal water, drops of Heaven's light, flew in all directions to the furthest reaches of dark space.

As they darted about, they swelled and grew in size. No longer did they resemble the waters of Heaven but became burning spheres of flame and heat shining brightly in the dark emptiness of space. As they sped to their mission's end, along the way many ceased their journey. Halting their passage, they hovered there in endless space making their eternal home where they hung. Some, as if growing too large and traveling too fast, broke into hundreds of pieces. Their light dimmed. Some took orbit and others tumbled through space in a slow graceful ballet. Others still, as if being pursued, continued beyond the sight of angel eyes and flew at the speed of Elohim's thoughts beyond all sight and knowledge. And the stars and planets and moons and all celestial beings took their ordained places and became lights for the coming ones.

And Elohim spoke again. "So shall my love be as the stars in the Heaven's for all my children beyond measure and counting without end. And these gifts shall be a witness to my love and my care and my sure hand. And secure they will be in the knowledge that greater is their maker than all that eye can see and ear hear. And though endless is the world and heavens that surround them, even greater is my being and my power and my love and compassion for them."

And as the countless stars in an endless heaven took their place, so even before the first of his children were born, was the love of Elohim declared. Elohim had taken a form and shape so all eyes could see. And even though Elohim, the three in one, was ever about the throne, still; Elohim was in all and above all and beyond all. All creation, all worlds, Heaven, Earth, space and time were but in the heart and mind of Elohim. For though he dwelt in a universe of man and angel, the universe was hidden in him.

A great light was perched beyond the Earth while satellites took orbit around it. And the moon too took its place to give light in the sky by night while the sun shone bright for mankind's waking days. The great canopy of water, ice and mist which roofed the Earth filtered the harsh light of the sun and amplified the light of the moon and stars. And the light from Elohim's hand that filled the Earth found its new source in sun and moon and distant star. The sun and moon gave a glow and warmth to all the Earth. And in the sky was the ever changing blush of colour and radiance - a canvas for the joy of all who would look to the heavens above.

Elohim's pleasure was great in the gift he created.

As the newborn Earth met its fifth day, Elohim spoke yet again; "Let there be." And the Spirit hovered still over the face of the seas and lakes and rivers and streams. And while resting in the sky above the waters, the Spirit of Elohim brought life at Elohim's bidding. And the seas became home to creature great and small, some so small no angel eyes could see. Some were so great, they would be called monsters in the eyes of man. And the seas and rivers abounded with life of every shape and size and colour.

And here did Elohim reveal his high art. Where Heaven's great craftsmen, even Lucifer, greatest artist of all, could cause in their craft the weeping of eyes and celebration of hearts, all paled and fell short of the magnificence seen not only in colour and shape and light but in life and movement.

And all that Elohim created was an intermingled tapestry of life. Each life existing not of itself but of parts and pieces and forces held together to make it whole. And each form of life could in no way command its own destiny for all had need of each other. And life itself was connected to the world in which it breathed and moved and by which it was nourished and protected. And a great connection of all things in creation was formed in an orchestration of life and world and elements. For all life lived to the benefit of all. One lived in need of the other. And all served the other in its very existence and purpose. Unity and diversity; reliance and harmony were Elohim's design reflecting his very heart: Father, Son and Spirit; three in one and one in three. And no life could ever know independence for all was in need of all.

Now here is the greatest mystery and wonder in all of creation; life would spawn life. And each generation of life and creature would owe its existence to the former. No life would come into being except that creature and creature reproduce, birthing generations of life under Elohim's guiding hand.

And the sky became the playground for creatures of flight that conquered the sky and air to soar and dance above the Earth to the wonder of all.

And in the twilight of this fifth day, Heaven's silence was broken. An uncontainable orchestra of song and verse and dance erupted. No voice was mute as all sang of the splendor witnessed in the world within and beneath the Crystal Lake. Then Lucifer raised his hands for order, but no instruction could be given or received to the unbridled enthusiasm of so many hearts abandoned to joy. Still every song blended in perfect harmony and verse. Reverence gave way to celebration and laughter. And then slowly the noise subsided. Celebration became concentration and anticipation once again. For Elohim was not finished the work he began. And the fifth day ended.

7

The Sixth Day

As the Earth spun toward the bright rays of the sun, a sixth day began for the new world. Elohim spoke once again the words of creation; "Let there be."

The life that came to the seas and waters of the Earth took hold now of the land in like manner. And the coloured deserts, the deep, rich forests and tree spiked mountains overflowed with life. And living, breathing, creeping things came upon the Earth. And creature great and small; wild and tame, fearsome and affable, walked and sprinted; crawled and crept; leapt and climbed.

And like the creatures of the sea, the creatures on the Earth were made for each other knitted together in an orchestration of life. And like creatures begat like creatures. Life sustained life and future generations would be born of the union of creature and creature all under the hand of Elohim.
And Elohim's high art could be seen in the life that covered the Earth. For beyond imagination were the diversity and variety; the complexity and simplicity and majesty of them all. There were creatures of beauty and grace and others awkward and

comical. Some were fragile and timid, yet others frightful to look upon. Mighty and stalwart, curious and delicate; huge and lumbering, peculiar and amusing were others. All extraordinary and astonishing. And Elohim was pleased for the gifts he had made were perfect and good.

In concert, the voice of Elohim resounded from the throne. Angels, more as if overhearing a conversation of Father to Son and Son to Spirit, heard his heart and words.

"Let us make mankind in our image," said Elohim. "Let us birth this day children of our own likeness. They shall resemble us in heart and form. And we shall set within them all they need to commune with their maker. We shall talk face to face and walk hand in hand. We shall make them male and female in our image. They shall be grafted into us and we shall be ever woven together with them. They shall live in unity and harmony with each other and with their father and creator. For in them is the treasure of my heart and the object of my love.

This day they shall ever mark for it is their beginning and they shall know and remember forever the end of all my desires. Out of one, we shall make two that the two might ever know their oneness and be as we are. For nothing shall separate them from me. And let no thing separate them from each other. They shall be man and wife, lover and friend, helpmate and helpmate. They shall be partners and coworkers equal in love and value and destiny."

Then Elohim came forth from the throne out of the fire and stepped into the new world setting his feet burning as fire on the Earth. Gabriel and Michael tentatively followed Elohim through the Crystal Sea into the new creation. With a host of other angels around them, they rested high in the sky above the Earth observing all that Elohim did. And as they hovered there, they sang ever so softly. The song was a song of creation and Earth was filled with the gentle and light symphony of angels. And as Elohim's feet touched the land, a garden of even greater beauty rose up around him and colour and hue and beauty knew no equal on this new Earth. The garden birthed a forest of trees and plants and flowers; and all kinds of growing things sprouted instantly around Elohim. And the trees were full of fruit and food and delicacy.

Elohim looked around the garden where there were paths and parks and places of rest and refreshing everywhere. And he was pleased.

Then Elohim spoke; "So shall this be the place of meeting where creator and creation forge love and friendship. Here shall a father walk with his children. Here shall his children cling to their father. For this truly is a garden for the growing. It shall be the place in which my children grow together in harmony and unity. And here shall they learn of me and see my heart and know all my ways. Daily, I will walk with them. I will speak with them and reveal to them the depths of my being. For this is Eden, the garden of love and intimacy. Here shall I grow a people wholly devoted to me.

This shall be their beginning but not their end, for their end shall be fully in my embrace. But here shall they taste of that which, one day, they shall feast on without limit or restraint.

Here in this place, shall we share time until all time is ours. Here in this garden, shall they see me and grow love in their hearts. Here in Eden, shall they know my goodness and grow to trust their maker. Here, shall their wills merge with mine with unity and purpose in their hearts. Here, shall their journey begin. And here, shall they choose love. We shall be one."

Now, Elohim stood in the center of the garden where there was a courtyard not made by hands. It was an open place from which paths led throughout the garden. Beyond the courtyard, both to the east and west, were two great rivers. One great river divided into four and the garden lay in the upper forks of the divide where the two great rivers came closest to each other. Now there were a number of streams that fed the garden. And on the edge of the clearing was a pool of water into which fell one of the streams. The gentle sound of rushing water was everywhere in Eden.

On the paths, Elohim walked as angels walked through the garden and his heart was glad, for it too was a good and acceptable gift. Now Elohim in a form more closely resembling angels walked beyond the garden and came to a place where the ground was rich but only shrubs and seedlings grew. The soil was fertile and black there. Bending low, he took the soil in his hand. Looking at it, he said; "This is Adam, the fabric of this Earth. Earth it is and from it shall all things grow. Its name is Adam, earth and soil. It is the womb of life. And it is neither beautiful nor grand in any fashion but humble beyond all. Still from this thing of little worth shall I forge a great treasure."

And in the palms of his hand, Elohim shaped and molded the moist earth into a form. And taking handful after handful of soil, he fashioned an image akin to angels and not unlike his own form which he took upon himself. The shape stood low and dark. Its features were vague without detail. And Elohim's hand gently stroked the mound of earth before him. And though it could not hear or understand his words, Elohim spoke to the earth.

"You are Adam," declared Elohim, "for you come from the earth. You are but humble soil. But within you will dwell the greatest of all treasures, my spirit, which today I give to you and all who come after you. And you shall be my first but not my last. For this day, I shall make mankind in my image, male and female, son and daughter. And you are great above all gifts from Elohim to Elohim. You and all your kind will be children to Elohim. You are fashioned this day by love and for love. And my love for you shall have no end. And there is none and no thing that will ever diminish my affection. For you shall have all my heart and no good thing will I keep from you. You are my child and children. You shall be my brother, my sister, my friend and my bride. You shall sit at my feet and walk by my side. For I shall be your inheritance."

Then Elohim breathed upon the form. Angels drew close to witness the birth of Elohim's children. Their song grew louder and louder. And the Spirit of Elohim as a whisper of mist flowed in and through and around the shape called Adam. And flesh came to the form and blood flowed through the form and the spirit of Elohim brought life and a soft glow of light to Adam. The spirit that entered into the man became his own and he became a living thing. Adam opened his eyes and with a huge gasp fell to his knees. His hands clung to the hands of Elohim. A soft radiance bloomed in his flesh.

Adam's second breath was no less violent. And gasping again he tried to stand. As Elohim reached down to support Adam, his appearance changed. The light that burned in him and through him and clouded his appearance subsided and the form of Elohim looked now little more than an angel in the sight of Adam.

Elohim appeared to Adam resembling Adam's own flesh but with greater radiance. Like a man of great stature clothed in bright white did Elohim appear. His whole being shone and as before his eyes burned brighter than the new sun, but were now, as well, soft and soothing as mist. As the first of Elohim's children glimpsed through newborn eyes the being of Elohim, tears streamed down Adam's face. Though not so clearly seen in those burning eyes, Elohim too wept tears of joy. Elohim drew Adam close into his arms as Adam shook and trembled. And Adam's first memory would always be of that embrace and the comfort and peace and rest he found there.

All that Elohim spoke to Adam, before his life began, was written on the walls of Adam's heart. Adam knew his worth and his purpose before ever he could stand without aid. Long they held each other in the new world. And when Adam could stand in his own strength before Elohim, he looked into those burning, soothing eyes and simply said, "Father."

And Adam knew his maker. His understanding was that of a man though his age could be measured in moments. Adam looked into the sky above him. And Elohim opened his eyes to see Heaven's light. A host of angels filled the sky above and around Adam. And he heard their song which was to Adam a joy unspeakable. The first music ever to fall on the ears of man was that of celebration. Though Adam could hear the music, he could not yet understand the words angels sang. For Elohim had not spoken to Adam in words at all but from heart to heart. And only later would Gabriel teach Adam and his equal the tongues of angels. And Adam did have a language but it was foreign to angel ears.

Now while Adam was still amazed and struck by the music surrounding him and the appearance of angels all around, Elohim took him by the hand. At the speed of thought, he brought Adam from that still barren place into the Garden of Eden. Adam wept for joy as he looked in astonishment at all that was around him. Having seen the barrenness of the Earth in that place beyond the garden where life was young, and now gazing upon the beauty and marvel of Eden, Adam saw what creation could be if only guided by a gentle, caring hand.

Adam, though new to the new world, had knowledge and understanding beyond measure. His hunger to learn was great, but great too was that which he was given to know at his birth.

For the next hours, Elohim and Adam simply walked and talked together. Adam had many questions though much he already knew. This walk and wandering with Elohim seemed natural and normal to Adam; hardly like his first introduction. For he knew much of Elohim, being created in his image. And the Spirit that was within Adam was so united with his creator and father, it scarcely seemed that Adam was only hours old. It felt to Adam that he had known Elohim for ages past. Still, he was but a babe in the new creation of which his vice-like mind was still very unaware.

After a time of wandering through the garden, Elohim with Adam by his side, came to the clearing in the center of the garden. There in the very center of the clearing were two trees. One was a sapling no taller than Adam himself and the other was a mature tree with the appearance of many years. And this tree was a fruit bearing tree not unlike the many other trees that surrounded the courtyard. It was in every manner the same as all other trees, but standing in such a prominent place caused Adam to wonder.

"Father," asked Adam; "what of these trees in the center of the garden?"

Elohim bent down to Adam and spoke face to face. "These trees" he said; "are like all trees in the garden. They bear fruit for the eating. Their fruit are good to the taste and can, like all fruit, nourish and strengthen you."

"Are they special trees that stand here for some other purpose? For in my heart, I sense these are unlike the other trees."

"Not entirely so my son," said Elohim. "They are the same and have no power or potential beyond all others I have given you. Their taste is no sweeter nor more bitter. They have no import beyond the simple fruit they bear. But they do, by my choosing, have purpose beyond the purpose of all other trees in this, your garden. And when this day is done, you shall know my design but for now it is enough to declare that the one bearing fruit is not for you or your kind. For a time, this tree shall stand as a trial, not to test what is in you, but to forge that which is not. So do not touch it my son. Do not eat from it. Do not desire it and do not give your mind reason to pursue interest in this one tree."

Adam looked at the tree and asked once more, "Father, why can I not…?"

Elohim interrupted him and touching Adam's head he smiled and said, "All is for you to know in due course and when you do not know, it is enough to know that I know."

Adam smiled and laughter took hold of him as he saw subtle humor in Elohim's words. Adam, now leaping and dancing around the courtyard, turned back to Elohim and smiling said, "I know you know and I know I need not know what you know." He laughed some more. Elohim too laughed at the innocent child before him who could find play in anything.

Now the angels' song, the sight of Elohim and the beauty of Eden was too great for Adam and he grew tired quickly and so Elohim caused Adam to fall into a deep sleep.

Now angels knew no sleep as man knows, though deep rest and refreshing was always theirs' for a time. And as Adam slept, angels pressed in to see this sight more closely. Many longed to touch the flesh of Adam for it was different than anything they had seen or known.

Unlike angel kind, who's all and everything, whose strength and nourishment came only from the light of Elohim which ever filled Heaven; Adam was in need of that which the world around him supplied. Adam's flesh craved the warmth of the sun. And Adam's body found nourishment in the eating of fruit and fig and the fare of the garden. And the waters in the garden were for Adam's drinking. Adam would grow tired and find new strength in but a few hours sleep. And in that sleep would the Spirit of Elohim come to Adam and bring comfort and strength again.

While Elohim was busy with Adam in the garden, angels drank in the delights of Eden and the new creation. And they were delirious with song and laughter as they gazed at Adam. Michael held to a fragile composure but his heart was bursting.

Gabriel, always at Elohim's side, cried tears of great joy as he gazed at his brother and kin Adam. And even more moved was he at the sight of Elohim whose subtle radiance was but a shadow of that which Heaven knew. Still the joy on Elohim's face shone brighter to Gabriel than a thousand suns.

Lucifer was of a different mind. He had difficulty seeing what others saw. His mind was full of questions and his heart gave little regard for these frail beings whose life was in their breath and whose fragile bodies relied on the world in which they lived. Lucifer observed only at a distance and would not abandon his post to leer at the new creature that so captured Heaven's attention. In an attempt to keep his host in order and at their duties, he forbade them to follow the other angels into the world of man.

And as Adam slept, Lucifer began a song louder than the song of angels still at play in the garden and the sky above the Earth. And in the recesses of Lucifer's mind, the music was meant to lure all the host back before the throne of Elohim for worship and celebration and song. His song had purpose other than to worship the King of Heaven and of the new Earth below. His desire was but to draw to himself the interest of Elohim and all of Heaven.

Lucifer sang of the greatness of Elohim, the three in one who sat above the throne. But Elohim found no joy in the song of Lucifer yet again. And Lucifer's attempt was disregarded by all even Elohim who would give no regard to the affliction in Lucifer's heart. For Lucifer that day knew jealousy, unknown in Heaven or in the heart of Elohim. None could see the secret device in his song, but Elohim knew it well.

As the pretense of Lucifer faded, he fell silent and all his host were with him. And none others took notice. Gabriel thought that Lucifer was simply silent as in reverence for the creation of the new world and the children of Elohim. Michael thought Lucifer was yet uncertain of his regained position and was silent in humble hesitation.

Lucifer felt little joy at the work of wonder before him, for he felt it was meant somehow to diminish him. And the rebuke of Elohim still stung in Lucifer's heart. Though restored for but a short while, he was uncertain as to the intent of Elohim and felt his position fragile. And so in Heaven that day, an angel brooded and contended in his heart over the children of Elohim. And though he knew it an error, he fed his mind with thoughts that fueled his passion. And there in the frenzied commotion of creation, Lucifer's heart turned back to his meditations of ill intent. And once again, threatening malice hung over him like a bird of prey.

Lucifer knew his mind and heart was as an open door and unbound scroll to Elohim. Even as he felt the firm grip of jealousy and knowing well that his mind was perched on the edge of peril, he spoke words of repentance. In unspoken words before the throne, he sought pardon once again. But though the words of his mind sought pardon, his deeper thoughts and desires betrayed him. And the Spirit of Elohim came upon him and he felt small and ashamed. While all in Heaven rejoiced, he could find no contentment, calm or comfort in that place. And so Lucifer in the midst of celebration asked leave to go and meditate and refresh himself. And permission was granted. Few, other than his own host, would notice his departure but Gabriel and Michael.

Michael noticed Lucifer's departure and turned to look to Elohim who still stood very close to his sleeping child. Elohim turned his head and glanced back toward Heaven. Michael came swiftly down and hovered over Adam, startling curious onlookers who scattered at the flurry. For no reason he could understand, Michael stood vigilant guard over this new creature. His light burned bright and his wings fell back, full and daunting. Michael's eyes flashed and moved alert with the stirring of every beast and angel.

"It's alright, Michael" spoke the gentile voice of Elohim heard only by Michael in his heart, "All is well."

Michael calmed and withdrew moving up and away from Adam. He hovered vigilantly and quietly above the scene of Father, son and a host of curious angels darting here and there.

Now Adam was in appearance a man of some age and stature and his mind was clear and bright without limit. And he was given the gift of speech both with the words of his mouth and the thoughts of his heart. For what he thought, Elohim knew and what Elohim thought, Adam knew. Where the tongues of angels were less than perfect but more than adequate, Adam's own speech was lesser still. But Adam, as with angels, knew in depth beyond whatever words his ears could hear.

And though Adam was a man true and not without understanding, he was still a child in heart. His mind had few limits but was as fallow ground, hungry for the seeds of knowledge. And to his rapidly growing knowledge, he had yet to learn wisdom and the wise use of that knowledge. And Elohim would be his teacher and the teacher of all his children yet to come. Gabriel too would aid mankind in these early days of creation.

On this sixth day of creation before the sun reached its height in the translucent sky, Elohim continued the perfection of his children.

8

The Eternal Bond

Now after Adam had slept for a brief time, he awoke to find Gabriel standing over him. Adam looked at the beauty and light that shone from this Prince of angels and looked to his own luminous skin. How different they were to Adam and he was taken by this creature in his heart.

"Adam," said the Archangel, "I am Gabriel, the servant of Elohim; Father, Son and Spirit. I am come to serve you and teach you many things that you may be full of the knowledge of Elohim. And Elohim himself will come to you each day and together you will grow in intimacy. And what a joy it will be to learn of him all the day. And what a delight for me to be now your teacher as you shall for a season be my young apprentice."

Now the first thing that Gabriel taught Adam was the tongue of angels and though Adam could speak his own tongue, it seemed too little and trite for true conversation especially with angels. Within the span of three hours Adam could speak the ancient tongue well and understood its every meaning. And his capacity for learning was without limit. Now perfect was Adam's memory as nothing escaped his mind once presented and embraced.

Later that day, the first of Adam's life, Elohim came into the midst of the garden and took Adam and walked with him. And the light that shone from Elohim was such joy for Adam and his words and voice were soothing and yet stirring. Elohim showed Adam his creation and explained his love and all these gifts to Adam. And Adam walked in constant awe.

But something in the heart of Adam provoked him, an indefinable ache and longing and he could not understand it. Like a deep splinter, he knew of its presence but could not remove it.

And Elohim said to Adam "What is this thing that pulls at you my son?"

"Father," said Adam, "I am too timid to say it but something seems not right. Some ache and longing is in me. I am ashamed for how can this be in your love and presence? For you have told me with your own words that I live to know you and to be your child. And my purpose is to grow with you in intimacy and fulfill my destiny at your side. Still it seems not enough. Am I somehow broken Father? Is there something incomplete in me? I feel strangely warped like a tree bent against the wind. I desire wholeness and straightness but feel my heart pushing against some unseen force and desire."

A smile and a glint of joy came over Elohim's face as if waiting and expecting Adam's question.

They stopped walking and turning to Adam, Elohim said; "I shall tell you of a wonder and mystery found in all my creation. You Adam have heard and marveled at the music of angels. In time you will discover the music in your own heart and learn the means to express it. You too shall become a skilful musician. An instrument of music is made for the playing but is incomplete without the player. Though it seems to the eye to be whole and complete, lacking nothing, it can never be whole and fulfilled until held in the hands of a skillful player. In this union is its purpose complete and its destiny fulfilled.

All around you, in all creation, there is no thing that abides on its own. All is a part of the life of another. For what is a tree but more than a tree. It is its roots and trunk and branches and leaves and the fruit of the tree are but a part of the whole. And the whole needs all its parts and each part needs the other and the whole as well. Such are you. You are whole, made in my image, but made of parts so connected and so aligned as to be one.

I have made you in my image. As I, you have a mind for reasoning and thinking, for remembering, for dialogue and discussion, for learning and valuing that which should be valued. But more than your thoughts and intelligence are you. You, like myself, have as well a will for the choosing, for freedom and for creating. Still with will and mind you are not whole, for I have given you a heart of emotions for laughing and weeping, to fear what should be feared and to rage at evil and injustice.

With all these, still you lack wholeness. I have given you my spirit which gives you life and light and makes you an eternal being of my kind. In this you are whole but still you are only part of yet another whole. For you are not complete without me. For without me, there is no life. And so together, we shall be as one father and son. Though it would seem there could be nothing more, you are still but a part.

This longing in you is set there by my hand. It is in you that you might seek and desire that which makes you whole. For now you still lack wholeness. As you are, you are still incomplete."

"Father," puzzled Adam, "what more could I long for and need that is not found in you? Surely, all you created in me must make me whole. What more is there?"

Elohim continued. "You are created my son to be part of my family and to love me, but your love is also prepared for another. What is in your heart is a good thing but as yet the fulfillment of all my plans for you has not arrived.

You are not meant to be alone. As of now, you remain disconnected like a flower without a stem. You are like a bird that lacks a wing and cannot fly nor soar though you long for the flight that you have never known.

This longing in your heart, I placed within you that you might desire and seek your wholeness in another. It is a pain and a hunger necessary and good. And this ache in you is to teach and tutor you. Mark this discomfort well Adam. For this reason I created you first and alone to stir in you this unease. For I never intended you to be without another. So desire wholeness and never choose this sore and unprofitable independence. For it is not good for mankind to be alone."

Adam amazed said, "I feel this longing, but I know not what I long for. What will make me whole?"

Elohim responded, "You are my son. This is true, but what is a son without a father but no son at all. The father makes the son and the son makes the father. You are made for me and I am yours, but you are made as well for another. You are to be a companion and lover, friend and helpmate, but you lack the same. These will you become when these you find."

Adam gasped at the words and thoughts of Elohim. In such excitement as he had yet known he asked "Father, I see I am not complete. It is in my very bones this ache and hunger. And where shall I find what you speak of in this world of delights? Surely they are plenty and for the taking. Shall I search for this other with all my heart? Is my companion near to me or in what far corner of this vast garden shall I find such treasure?"

Elohim spoke; "So little have you seen Adam in your first hours of life. Do you think you shall find this treasure here in this garden? And of what you have seen is there anything that brings you such delight so as to quell your hunger and lack? What in this place shall bring you wholeness do you think?"

"I do not know Father," said Adam "but as I am a being of breath and flesh and bone, it must be that one of these creatures here in the garden are indeed created for me and I for them. And many are the creatures in the garden. But I have seen so few as yet and each one is a wonder to me. So far, I do not see a companion for me to quench the thirst in my heart."

"Shall I aid you in the seeking?" asked Elohim.

There was on Elohim's face a lighthearted expression and one of playful sport.

"Yes Father, please," burst Adam.

Elohim took Adam to the center clearing in the middle of the garden where several paths converged. And there, Gabriel was waiting. With a nod and a motion Gabriel waived his hands and unseen to Adam a host of angels flew about the garden and in the world beyond.

Adam first heard it as the crackling of leaves and branches under many feet but soon the air was filled with a clamor of noise, squawks and screeches, yips and yells and howls and roars. And the forest of trees and bushes that encircled the clearing seemed to come alive moving and rocking. Then one by one and in dozens and hundreds, creatures burst into the open. Adam took a step behind Elohim. Gabriel and Elohim began to laugh. It was a sight unseen and even angels laughed aloud as creatures of every sort poured into the clearing until hardly was there room for another.

Elohim turned to Adam and still laughing said, "What do you think of these Adam?"

Adam too laughed, a somewhat apprehensive laugh, as he was overwhelmed at the beasts that stood around him.

"They are marvelous, wonderful," said Adam. "Marvelous. I have seen a few of these before. This one here with the tall ears; I know it well in only the last hours. What is it and what are all these called? Wonderful! Amazing!"

Adam in his excitement began to repeat himself and his talk quickened for he was astonished;

"Wonderful, what are they all called?" Adam asked "Tell me their names. What do you call them? I am eager to know them. Look at the nose on that one there. It is so long. And those there that fly. What beauty. Wonderful, so marvelous."

Adam began to walk through the menagerie before him touching them and laughing.

He looked back at Elohim and asked; "What are their names? What shall I call them? How many of them are there? I do not see two the same."

"Calm," said Elohim. "You are thrilled to the brim and I am happy to see you so. Come to me my son. You will have much time to see and play and know."

Adam walked slowly back to Elohim but could not take his eyes off the many beasts and creatures that roamed now in close quarters around the garden.

"They have no names as yet" said Elohim "for they are your possessions as are all things your eyes can see. And as they are your possessions, you have the right to name them. And the naming of these beasts and creatures shall be a sign that they are yours to own and rule over. They belong to you and those who come after you and what you call them so shall they be."

"Mine?" asked Adam. "All of them?"

"These are but a few" said Elohim. "There are many more of similar kind and some of slight variation, smaller, larger, of different hue and colour. But here in this place is one of all, a token of the rest."

Adam walked through the opening in the middle of the garden and touching each one he called it by its name. Now in the newborn language of man, which lacked the eloquence and imagination of angels tongue, Adam in childlike expression called them by that which his eyes could see. And each and every outstanding feature of the beast became its name.

And so that beast which bent its head to eat the grass of the garden was called in the infant language of man "grass eater." And for the next that ate its food likewise, it was called "bowed to the ground." And yet the next was "with head hung low." A great beast of girth and length was simply called the "enormous one." One that sprouted great horns became "tusk bearer." The language of mankind would grow with man and be greatly aided by angels. And so the names of beasts and creatures would change and grow as well. But in these early hours of life, Adam found a name for all living things that eye could see and hand could touch.

Adam looked out over the throng of gathered beasts and turning to Elohim, a look of disappointment was clear on his face.

"Father, are there more yet to see that I have not seen?" asked Adam.

"No, my son," said Elohim "this is all for now. But creation continues. It is a power and force that shall never stop."

"Father, do I dishonor you to find no companion in your great and wonderful work before me? For my eye and heart see no such being that can indeed join me in my life as you and I are joined."

"On the contrary my son," said Elohim. "I am not disappointed at all. This is a lesson for you to learn. And in the learning you honor me. In your seeking, you have not found because there is nothing yet to find. That which you lack as yet has no life. And now share your heart with me my son. What have you learned in this pursuit of that which you cannot find?"

"That no creature is like myself or equal to my being," said Adam. "For I am a shadow of Elohim made in his likeness to be his child. Great these creatures are but none share the light of Elohim in their flesh or the spirit of Elohim in their hearts. Though great joy they can bring, they can in no way be as I am and join with me."

"Though so young, you are so wise even now my son," said Elohim. "For you have learned a lesson that shall be for you and your kin from generation to generation that you are unique in this creation. By design and purpose, there is none like you. You are unique, created in my image for the highest of all purposes and never will you find fullness apart from others of equal value and design and purpose. For this is my first and great proclamation to you and all your generations that it is not good for mankind to be alone. In my creation, which is a gift to you, you shall know great joy and pleasure. But fragile it will be compared to the joy you shall find in your own kind. And you shall find no great and lasting comfort or peace in that which is not of your own kind. For you are not of yourself but you will always belong to another and another. It is not good for mankind to be alone."

Exhausted, Adam sat on the ground as he tried to take in the words of Elohim. For the mystery was too great for him. But in those words, he found a hope in that which his mind could not hold. And Adam slept once again.

Now Elohim did not bend again to the earth but reached into Adam and took from his flesh a piece of bone. And laying it next to Adam, he breathed upon the shard of bone from Adam's side. And the bone began to grow and take shape. And flesh and blood came to the shape and the light of Elohim glowed bright in the form beside Adam. And in like fashion, this new creature came to life and gasped its first breath of air in the new world. And she too clung to Elohim until she found her own strength and could stand unaided. And tears were wept by all even angels who silently hung in the sky around the new creation and the children of Elohim.

Elohim spoke to the new creation; "You are Eve, daughter of my heart and mother of all the Earth and all and every generation of my children. You are created for me and I am for you. And I shall be your father and you my daughter. For in you is my likeness and my spirit and you are a reflection of my heart and my heart's desire. And all the days of your life shall you love me and walk with me. And we shall grow together in unity and love. We shall be one and together for all eternity. And you shall have all my heart and all my love and you shall lack no good thing for I am your inheritance. You are Eve and all life shall owe its life to you."

And Eve looked into the eyes of Elohim and simply said, "Father."

Elohim held Eve in his arms while Adam slept. And as Eve felt the embrace of Elohim, she knew a bliss and a comfort and peace that would be the strength of her life. And she longed to stay in those arms and to gaze into the bright but soothing eyes of Elohim. After a time, she turned outward and gazed upon the garden around her and her heart knew beauty for her heart was made for such. And all that Elohim had spoken to Adam he spoke to her and she knew her great purpose and all the heart of Elohim. And she too was amazed at all of creation. Sight and sound and every delight brought laughter and tears.

Now Eve stood over Adam in amazement as he slept. And with her eyes discovered every part of him and wondered at the discovery. Then she reached down and touched his olive face. Elohim was slow to explain this creature before her.

"Father, I see this great being before me and I know it is like me. And it is beautiful and desirable beyond all that I can see."

And Elohim stretched out his hands and opened the vale of Heaven to Eve's eyes. The light of Heaven pierced the frail light of the Earth below and myriads of angels hovered around her and far off. And in an instant all the beauty of Heaven and Earth were before her, too great for her eyes or heart to behold. She bowed her head to the ground and gasped for air as if she could find none.

Elohim bent close to her ear and spoke in a whisper; "So great is my love for you," he said. "It has no limits and no end. And all of creation, Heaven and Earth, are pale in my heart compared with you. All my creation is for you, your own possession. But here at your feet still in slumber is a gift that will ever declare my love for you. It is the greatest of all my gifts. The summit of my love for you is found here beneath your feet. For this is Adam and he, like you, above all things is the treasure of my heart. He is for you and you are as well a gift for him. For you are the same and one."

Eve almost ignoring the brilliant vision of Heaven's open gate, bent low and sat stroking the sleeping face of Adam.

"My daughter," continued Elohim, "you shall know the love of a man and of a husband; of a friend and a partner; of sister and brother. And to you who are dear to my heart is given a great marvel and mystery which Adam and his brothers can never know. You shall know the joy of creation. We together shall birth new and wondrous treasures in the children of our hearts. They shall be your greatest heart's desire. The fruit of your union with Adam shall be children and family; more and greater intimacy. You shall birth treasures upon the Earth until the whole Earth is filled with the children of Elohim. And we shall all be one and together for all eternity."

As Eve looked to Adam, she could see straight into his heart and was touched by his spirit as he lay there. And she knew a deep love for Adam before he ever spoke to her.

Now, Elohim stirred Adam who nearly jumped at the sight of Eve and he too touched her spirit and knew her heart. And such a treasure was she that his love extended beyond all measure. In his young heart in his first hours of life, he now knew two great loves, that for his father and now a new and deep love for his bride.

Adam and Eve found each other in that moment and fell into each other's arms. And tears of joy and comfort flowed in that first embrace. Adam stroked the brown and shining hair of Eve. It was like silk to the touch and a fragrance was about her, refreshing and pleasant beyond even the fragrance that filled the garden. And Eve felt the strength of Adam's arms around her; a strength beyond her own and calm and peace was full in those arms. Elohim smiled and sang a song of joy ever so softly while angels sighed and fainted at the sight of Earth's first great love.

And Elohim spoke to all of Heaven and to his new children; "For this reason shall a man leave his house and home, his mother and father and cling and cleave to his wife and partner. And daughter shall leave her abode of youthful comfort and make her home with her husband until they too become the home and house and mother and father of another and another and so shall it be from generation to generation."

Adam turned to Eve and said, "Bone of my bone and flesh of my flesh. We are the same, you and I; both made in the likeness and image of our father. We are of the same substance crafted by his hand. This day we are one flesh and will walk one path and serve one and the same purpose - to be his children. We will enter into the joy of true companionship forever and ever.

We shall be one as Elohim is one; you in I, and I in you, and we both in the Father. We are family and kin, his children and his heirs made for his heart and made for each other. We are equals you and I and equally unique. I am your helpmate and you are mine and together, we shall rule this Earth and fulfill all his great purposes."

Eve in turn spoke to Adam. "In you is his light and his spirit as in I. Equals and partners we are. And I shall ever love and desire you. I shall be your friend and partner in all things and together we shall nurture and cultivate this garden, this Earth and the family of Elohim from generation to generation. And our love shall spread across this creation from end to end like the light of the sun. And we shall fulfill all his heart's desires and bring to him a world of treasures; children for the Father."

Elohim spoke now not only to Adam and Eve but to all creation and all of Heaven above. And his voice could be heard by every creature on the Earth and every angel in even the far reaches of Heaven. And his tone was one of strength and authority and less the gentle father Adam and Eve had known. "You my children," declared Elohim, "shall rule over all my creation here in this world. For you are my heirs and joint heirs and all authority I give to you in this realm of Earth. And you shall be instruments of my will and my heart's desire in this place. You shall stand as kings over all. And you shall rule and lead and command all things and all life and every creature great and small. Every crawling, creeping, living, breathing thing shall be under your authority. And as kings, you shall extend my kingdom and my household and my family in this realm.

So, be fruitful and multiply and bear sons and daughters, princes and princesses, kings and queens to rule throughout all this realm from generation to generation. And let every generation see the greatness and wonder of Elohim and his children.

As for this Earth, work to bring it to its full fruition. For mysteries and treasures and wonders are for the discovering. And to all that I have begun you shall add. Every seed I have planted you shall harvest. Fulfill the destiny of this world. Cultivate its every potential. Build, create, discover and uncover all that is hidden. Reign and rule over all. Cover the Earth with the children of Elohim and cover it well with the knowledge of the most high. This is a gift from me to all my children for all generations."

All of Heaven sang. But not all, for there was one who brooded and sighed and grumbled alone in a far corner of Heaven while all others with lightened hearts sang and celebrated.

9

The Two Trees

And now in the last hours of light on this sixth day, Elohim once again stood with his children in the courtyard of the garden. Standing before the two trees, he spoke all his heart concerning them.

"My children," said Elohim, stretching out his hand and touching the larger of the two trees; "this is the tree of the Knowledge of Good and Evil. You shall not touch it, nor eat from it. Though all is yours, this one thing I shall deny you for a time. For you are mine, created in my image and you lack nothing. But you are much like this tree young and new to the world. You have need to grow and mature and bring forth fruit as well.

As of now, you know only in part my heart for you. My love is forever and I am forever for you. But I desire that you as well choose to love and value me for all time. Love is not love unless freedom makes it so. You are free to love me but as well free to choose other than the love you were created for.

This tree has no properties that you should find desirable, but should you choose this tree then it shall be against my will and my desires. And to choose other than I is to choose other than love. That which is not love is evil."

Elohim turned and knelt before his children. His eyes burned bright as he looked into theirs. And though bright as the sun, they turned not away from his gaze but found soothing comfort and joyful peace.

Elohim continued; "Though this tree has no power in itself, your will has the power of life and death. Do not go the way of this tree. For the day that you choose evil over love; this tree over my heart's desire; your will over my will, that day you shall know evil and it shall take hold of you. And that day you shall know death and pain and by the steerage of your own wills shall we be separated - your heart from my heart, your purpose from my purpose."

Adam and Eve took several quick steps away from the tree but could not take their eyes off of it.

"Father," said Eve. "Take it away!"

Adam of like mind followed Eve's words. "We do not want it here in this place. We are yours and always will be. Remove it Father, take it far from us and far from this our garden."

"This I cannot do," sighed Elohim.

"Do not worry my children. For there is no power of enticement in this tree. It need not be a fearful thing. It will not move you or call to you in any fashion. It is but a tree. This tree is like a door through which you must never walk for to do so is death and evil. But you still rule here in this place even over this tree. This tree offers you no more than a terrible occasion to choose evil. The power is not in the tree but in your hearts.

For your will and freedom must have opportunity or there is no freedom at all. And if no freedom then there is no love. You are not a stone or a tree or a bird or any other creature that lives to live. You live to love and be loved. And so you must eternally choose all that is good and valuable and worth loving. But if your freedom is bound by the lack of opportunity, then you are little more than stone or animal. Love is found in that which you treasure and value the most. This day, I am the treasure of your heart and you are mine. Let your heart always desire what you treasure. For everything that you are flows from the treasure of your heart. Guard that most precious treasure and accept no other of lesser value. Each and every day choose to love what is in your heart to love.

And now open your eyes and see that there is no value or treasure in this tree. Know that to oppose my loving desires for you is to oppose your very purpose and cast aside the highest of all destinies.

This tree is for your freedom not for malice. Choose love. Choose it today and tomorrow and the next. And with every passing day, this tree shall whither and die by your choosing. Above all things value our love and pursue me to your heart's content. The tree shall take care of itself.

Deny this opportunity and refuse it. This day and all others, let your heart say 'yes' to me your father and say in your heart 'no' to this tree. For your resolute will shall kill opportunity, then no more shall this tree stand in the garden and no thing shall I withhold from you ever again. And in that place of final victory, we shall be one and no thought will ever enter your mind to lure you from my love. Love shall be safe and never know the threat that now abides with this tree."

Adam and Eve looked at the tree still with worried expressions on their faces.

Elohim continued, "Do not worry my precious little ones. This is a good thing to shape and mold your character and your destiny. And in the forging of your destiny, we are partners. I shall do my part to love and stir you in that love, and you shall do your part to abide in my will until your character and your will reflects mine. This is your destiny to be one with me.

Here and now in your youthful innocence, what you desire you now choose, but here is wisdom for generations, what you choose shall also shape your desires.

I have chosen a path for you. And I am on that path and in that path. It is a path of life and relationship, of intimacy and joy. Never stray from it. Though I can lay a path before you, it is you who must walk that path."

Elohim moved over to the smaller sapling that stood only meters away from the other tree.

"Now behold the Tree of Life. This tree is yet to bear fruit but soon it will do so. Each day, it shall grow until it bears a fruit from which you shall eat. The death of the one shall bring life to the other. This too is in your hands. This day I set before you life and death - choose life. This Tree of Life will complete what I have begun in you. For in the eating of its fruit you shall know a new measure of life. You shall be changed in your bodies and become as angels who are free to enjoy the pleasures of creation but are not confined by its borders and boundaries.

Your bodies are frail for a time and your mind and spirit are its captives. But when the tree of the Knowledge of Good and Evil diminishes and dies, this Tree of Life shall mature, and one shall replace the other. And in a great celebration as yet to be seen in all of Heaven, you shall eat from this tree and become one with the Father and Son and Spirit. And fully shall you know the embrace of Elohim. And you shall rule both Heaven and Earth by my side. You shall even govern angels and new worlds."

Adam and Eve's heads spun as Elohim spoke in such depths about the two trees in the courtyard. And they grew tired. With an embrace and a kiss, Elohim bid them farewell and departed though he was always there and everywhere.

Elohim's last words to them and to all on that day were simply;

"All is good, very, very good."

As dusk settled over the garden on this mankind's first day, Adam and Eve walked and talked together. Adam shared with Eve all that had happened and all he had learned in those few hours before her birth. As great and beautiful as creation was around them, they were more enraptured with each other.

They stopped their progress often, just to stare and look into each others eyes. And in the looking, they found themselves laughing without cause. Walking down a path that led far from the courtyard they came to a calm lake of emerald. The lake was as glass except for the ripples that tumbled toward the shore when occasional curious creatures popped through the surface for a breath of warm and moist air.

As the sun fell deep into a grove of tall standing trees, soft arrows of light shot through brown and grey pillars in all directions. After stopping for a while to take in the dance of light, Eve turned to Adam and with great emotion in her voice said, "Adam, we are the same and equal, you and I, but we are so very different. In you, I see strengths and gifts given by Elohim that I do not myself possess. I lack much of what I see in you."

"Yes!" said Adam. "I understand. For that which I cannot find in myself, I see brightly shining in you. In you is greater vision to see what I cannot see. You understand this garden differently than I. There are many things I cannot see with my eyes, understand with my mind nor feel with my heart. They are lost to me unless you aid me in the discovery. What you see and know and feel you show me through your words."

"Eve," said Adam. "I need you. I lack the things you have and need your gifts. Now I understand what Elohim means in giving you to me and me to you. For together we are more and better than ever we could be apart.

And this, Eve, you do not truly know. But Elohim created me first in order to teach me what every man must know. Before you were birthed from my flesh, for a brief time, I was indeed alone. I had not my equal to love and hold. And there in that place, before we were joined in heart and spirit, I was unfulfilled. And even in the presence of Elohim, part of me was alone. I felt incomplete. I could not see what it was I lacked and needed until now."

Eve looked deep into the eyes of Adam and responded; "I do not know of that which you speak. For I know only my brief time with you and cannot imagine a world without you. I only see that we are made for each other. Our very differences knit our hearts together. Love, I see is a hunger and I, my husband and friend, hunger for you. I long for your presence and your touch and the sound of your voice. I desire to be near the very heart of you. For you complete what is lacking in me. For this has Elohim made us the same and yet not the same - to be truly one and always in need of the other."

They continued to walk through the garden but frequently interrupted their journey stopping to embrace and hold each other for long periods of time. Adam shared with Eve the names of those animals they came across in their wanderings.

They sat in a bright green patch of soft moss and watched for the first time the sun slide behind rolling hills of orange and purple. And as it slipped away, the skies above lit up as light exploded through an opaque misty horizon. The full moon hung over their shoulders catching the light of the disappearing sun, eager for its chance to conquer the gentle evening sky.

Gabriel stood a short ways off watching their every move. Michael hovered unseen above the two lovers in the moss. Night fell and the sixth day of creation was no more.

The next morning Gabriel still sat in the garden having watched Adam and Eve through the night. The angel began to sing as the sun rose on this its seventh day. Adam and Eve woke to the sound of angel song and embraced each other once again. Gabriel smiled as Adam and Eve approached slowly and silently not wanting to disturb his music.

"Good morning Seed of Elohim and Monarchs of all the Earth," said Gabriel, not looking at the two who stood curiously at a distance.

After a moment, Gabriel rose from the ground and turned toward the children of Elohim. He stood a full meter above Adam, the tallest of the two.

"Should I be so privileged as to call you friends and brothers?"

"Indeed," said Eve. "For I see the light of Elohim in your eyes, Prince of angels, and strong is his love and Spirit in you."

"Honored are we to have you love us so and we shall always love that which Elohim loves. You are friend and brother," said Adam.

Like long lost friends, the three embraced.

"Today" said Gabriel "is a day of rest and refreshing and celebration. For Elohim's dream is no longer a dream but a longing fulfilled."

The pleasure and joy of Elohim was everywhere and could be felt as easily as the cool mist that rose from fissures in the ground throughout the whole of the garden. For Elohim was finished and all that he had created was good in his eyes.

Gabriel spent the day with Adam and Eve and taught them many things and answered many questions. And all that day, there was rest and peace and celebration. Unseen angels hovered above the Earth singing songs of praise and honor to Elohim. And the songs proclaimed how good and wondrous was the creation of the world and all things in it. And there was constant celebration over the children of Elohim, the treasure of his heart.

Now, it was Elohim's great desire and plan, when creation was done, to daily walk with his children down the paths of the garden, resting at times with them by the quiet pools. And they would ask many questions and grow in understanding until able to fathom the deepest truths. Gabriel too was summoned by Elohim to come into the garden and guide them in paths of understanding and wisdom. And day after day, Adam and Eve grew together in heart and mind.

Each day at a particular hour, Elohim would come to walk with them in the garden and together they would talk of many things. Though Elohim's presence was everywhere and Adam and Eve could speak to him at all times, he appeared daily in the form of his choosing, which was most like angels. This was the greatest joy of the day for Adam and Eve. For then they could touch him and hold him and look into his eyes. Everyday, they would laugh and tremble together as they eagerly waited for Elohim to appear. For he was their father true and they were expectant children eagerly waiting for this daily reunion.

And each day they took little notice of the Tree of the Knowledge of Good and Evil. And day by day the tree began to look less vibrant and more and more sickly.

One day, Adam called to Eve to see a wonder in the courtyard. The Tree of Life had grown and buds were sprouting from its branches. It would be a short while until it would bear fruit.

10

The Rise of Darkness

Now the time of man is not like the time of angels. For though Heaven knows time, it is not measured in hours and days nor the rising of the sun or the passing of seasons. For although angels walk in time, its passing can seem slower or faster. It can seem to hang unmoving without event or occurrence.

As time passed upon the Earth, Lucifer remained in his self imposed exile in a garden in the far corner of Heaven.

There was in the legions assigned to Lucifer a great General of angels whose name was Gia. And Gia knew all the thoughts of Lucifer and felt much as Lucifer felt.

Now, there were in Heaven many kinds of angels, and though of the same substance, they were different in appearance and gifts and talents, each being crafted for their purpose. Some were great in strength and size while others were slight and graceful creatures. Now the ranks of lesser angels were not as Archangels. For Archangels were by design and nature free beings created for high purposes and service. They were creatures of free mind and free wills and full of emotion and affections. Though crafted for service, they were still creatures of love and passion and strength of mind and will.

Lesser ranks had lesser freedom. Like creatures of flesh in the new world, some were bound as if by instinct to their duties while others knew only partial freedom and could not but fulfill their destiny as if by compulsion - a driving instinct of sorts. Still there was a level of freedom within their assigned duties. And the host assigned to Lucifer were of various sorts. Some would serve him and follow him by design as they were created to do so by the hand of Elohim. Others had greater freedom, but still were created to follow and serve their Prince of angels.

Now Gia was an angel of great freedom. But still in him were the seeds of servitude. He could not imagine anything other than being true to his master. And though free to do what was good in his own eyes, he continually chose loyalty to one who was less than loyal. The allegiance to his Lord Lucifer was great and unshakable. And in the midst of Lucifer's earlier correction, Gia felt also the sting of Elohim's rebuke. And his heart had compassion for Lucifer.

Now Gia sought out Lucifer in a far corner of Heaven and came upon him unawares. And Lucifer turned to see who was behind him and was caught off guard by Gia.

"My Lord," said Gia, "what troubles you so? Are you still in mourning over a loss now all but forgotten. Have you not regained all that was rightfully yours? And are you not still all you ever were?"

"And what is it that you think I am and was?" said Lucifer. "For little it is that I am restored when all of Heaven rejoices over beings too frail for beauty and too meek for greatness. And while Heaven is captivated with Elohim's recent pursuit, I am diminished. And why do I not rejoice as all others do, nor love and value that which is loved and valued by all? Am I not the great artist who sees and knows the very nature of beauty? And here in this place am I now excluded and estranged from Heaven's delight and the joy of all? For I do not see in these creatures reason for such clamor."

"My Lord," said Gia, whose blind devotion in his heart bred a foul flattery in his tongue.

"Why do you scorn yourself so? Now you have need to see and know as I see and know. For my eyes are not dimmed by the rebuke of Elohim and my opinions are steady and constant. You are who you have always been. And I am in awe of your greatness. What scheme is this in your heart to rob you of your privileged place and true worth? Think not these unworthy thoughts but come to know Lucifer as I know him. And honor him with all the honor he deserves for he is the likeness of Elohim and the beauty of all Heaven. None other can take from him all that has been placed into his hands. Revive yourself my Lord and show yourself strong. For your light shall yet shine for all to see."

Lucifer's head rose up to meet the eyes of Gia.

"My servant," he said "your loyalty is a sure thing. I fear my thoughts and imaginations have drawn me to a foreign place and my mind and heart may not know the way back. I know I should abandon these thoughts and return to reason and be right again in the eyes of all. But I have not the will to do so. For though it is a certainty that my post will no longer be mine once again, I shall, I think, in no way depart from my destiny. Elohim is no fool and he knows that I have wandered from his will and desires. And when the uproar of his new creation subsides, I will lose my place once more and you may sit yet at the side of another master."

"May it never be Lord," said Gia. "For you are Lucifer and now your eyes are clouded and your vision is blurred. Your heart is bound and your will is bent. And who has done this to you? None but yourself. Surely, Elohim has yet purpose for you. Your post can never be filled by any other than the one designed to fill it.

And what of your post and privilege? Is that so grand to you after all? Even if you were to join the lesser world of man and never see Heaven again, are you not still the shining one, the perfect one? Your place and position cannot diminish you. Will you not always be as you are? And in better times, I have heard you say that you shall be even greater. I have known all your mind and not so long ago did you declare your freedom to me. And of your freedom I have marveled. It is a wonder to me.

Now let me ask you of that which you have so loudly proclaimed. Are you not free? And if you are created free than where does that freedom lead you? Perhaps beyond the station you so vigorously covet. And now take hold of yourself and show me your freedom. These recent contrary thoughts have not the power to diminish your true self, but your will does indeed have the power to forge a destiny of your choosing. I do not believe that Elohim has forsaken you for never would he do so. Do not now deny yourself."

Gia continued with many words to elevate Lucifer in his own mind and as Lucifer heard his own thoughts through the lips of another, flattery found its mark. Lucifer raised his head and his voice to match. His disposition changed and his demeanor became bold and imposing. A light of twisted revelation flashed through his mind and he felt illuminated by his old imaginations. And as he turned to Gia, his eyes were burning bright and a smile was on his face.

Behind Gia, some distance off, was the host of Lucifer. For they had followed Gia and watching and listening, they drew ever closer. And Lucifer found there an unexpected audience to which he could unfold his ambitions.

Gia continued his exaltation of Lucifer; "Are you not great in the eyes of all and will you not always be so?"

Lucifer cut short Gia's praise.

"And more than great!" said Lucifer. "For position and post do not define my value or worth. Can another know me better than myself? I am Lucifer and now I see that I am great and cannot be diminished by any other, neither creature nor creator. Gia, your words are true, beyond your knowledge, for I am who I am. And I shall be more.

Too long have I been burdened with a false and groundless guilt. For there never was any harm or wrong in the wonderings of my thoughts. I have always honored Elohim but honor for me has been denied. I will no longer deny my true self or what I will be. And honor I shall have. For it is my destiny to become that which I am not as yet. Though I am created, I have been given life and purpose and my life and purpose are my own. I did not by my own design come to be but by his hand. And his hand has perfected me and the gift in me grows to an even greater perfection. It is no longer his for he has withdrawn his hand. And what I am and will be is now in my own hands. He has relinquished all my being and destiny to me.

Though Elohim's hand stoked the fires of my life, I burn bright by all that I possess. Does not Heaven shine with the art of my hand and does not all of Heaven sing the songs of my heart. And if Heaven is made greater by my craft, than is not Heaven mine as well as his? For though he set stone upon stone and raised Heaven's walls, I have filled it with light and life and beauty for all. For we are allies, Elohim and I, each adding to the others best. And if there is justice then Heaven shall be mine and my reward as well. Selfless I have toiled and eager I have served for the good of all. So why does all of Heaven seek to hinder what Elohim has begun in me?

Do I see that there is mischief in the suppression of my greatness and true value? For I now see clearly that the birth of man is a device to turn all of Heaven away from me. Is there in this place a repression of my freedom and a hand of tyranny over my destiny? Does he now repent of all he has caused me to be? But perhaps by clever words and sweet speech am I enticed to forge a prison for myself. And for a short while was I willing to suffer loss and injury."

Lucifer laughed out loud and even Gia who intended to raise Lucifer from his sadness was surprised to find such bluster in his master.

Lucifer continued, "Will he now turn his head from his greatest creation? I think not. Elohim was my beginning. I asked not for it. But now, I am Lucifer and my beginning does not determine my end. And if I desire greatness, as no other in Heaven deserves, then the post and position he offers me grows too little for me. It is not befitting who I am nor what I shall become in due course. For position and title and rank, which matter very little to me, are granted in great measure to those who warrant the claim. I deserve more than any position and rank that can be awarded. For Heaven is my home and my domain. So should Heaven be mine as well. So great is Heaven it is easily shared and ruled by two masters. Then I shall bestow rank and honor and position on those whom I deem deserving.

And if Heaven is too much to share with such a worthy ally and commendable friend as I then Elohim should create for me a domain of surpassing value.

Elohim has called me "rival." But never was there rivalry in my heart. That false and…"

Lucifer hesitated. "…regretful. Yes! That regretful charge still stings in my heart. But though it be false, I am assured by my accuser that there can be in him no rivalry toward me. For how could there dwell in Elohim's heart that which he has falsely condemned in me. I am no rival. I am the fulfillment of his great work and the evolution of his perfect design. And so shall he delight to render unto me all I desire. If Elohim be true, and so he must be, then he shall find my claim innocent and just and well merited.

For I shall be as Elohim. The creation shall by the creator's design become as the creator himself. And we shall speak face to face and heart to heart. And though he would injure me in my suppression, I shall rise above the offense and call him friend and equal and hosts of angels shall see the majesty of Elohim and Lucifer.

And if he be who he says he is then this he shall grant without hesitancy. And in this shall he find joy. For I shall become what is beyond his intention but true to his design. A grateful and good partner and companion I shall be; but servant to none. For I too am master.

I shall become like the most high Elohim and his embrace shall he extend to me as I extend it to lesser beings. Michael and Gabriel shall find a benevolent master in me. Grateful will they be to serve at my feet and to gaze upon my beauty. I shall perfect my craft and teach it to the multitudes who will in turn give gifts of worship and praise to Lucifer, the shining one. And Elohim shall be pleased at the work of his hand.

He should not deny me this destiny for to do so is to deny himself and his love for me. His humility shall not fail him in this. And I shall never seek his mercy again, for there can be no offence in the path I have chosen. I aspire only to share what he surely is willing to share with me. He shall see that his device to keep me from my full potential was not in his best interests. And he shall repent of any harm he has caused me. For I know his character. And if he longs to uphold it then this he shall grant me, freedom to reach my highest at his side with no peril to his glory and honor. In this I am confident. I will be as the most high Elohim."

Now Lucifer heard the sound of trumpets in the distance and all of Heaven seemed to be on the move. The song of celebration had stopped. A deep and profound silence hung in Heaven's air and all that could be heard was the growing echo of the trumpets. And behind the trumpets came other sounds of flight and fury.

Gia stood in disbelief at the words of his master though his own flattery and blind support had encouraged it. Still he was his master's servant. He turned to Lucifer and cried, "All of Heaven is stirred and moving and the song has ceased. I hear them coming and the wings of Michael are loud and furious. He approaches. What shall I do, my Lord?"

Lucifer stretched out his arms, raised his head and with a loud voice he sang and summoned his host to his side. For they all had followed Gia and stood in waiting but a little way off. Lucifer turned to Gia and cried out, "Who is for me?"

Gia at the speed of thought surveyed the hearts and minds of the host. For all were well acquainted with the many thoughts and imaginations in the heart of their master. And even before the rebuke of Elohim, many had been wooed to their master's service beyond all reason. Such was the enticement of Lucifer's art and craft.

In less than a heartbeat Gia's challenge to the host was set forth. "Now is the time! Stand with us or stand against us!"

Though some of higher rank fled back to the citadel of Elohim, most who surrendered their wills to Lucifer stood their ground and in silence aligned themselves to Lucifer. And with all their hearts they embraced his ambition. And though they knew not what would happen, they trusted Lucifer's proclamation of self-governance and felt it agreeable, with an unspoken promise of great rewards for themselves. For the unease and discontentment of Lucifer long invaded their hearts and turned their wills first and foremost to Lucifer above and beyond their devotion to Elohim. But never before was the devotion of their heart tried and tested till this desperate hour.

While a few fled crying out for Elohim, a myriad of angels took their place behind Lucifer. Gia and a lesser contingent of great and powerful angels,

Lords and Generals, stood at their master's side. Lucifer mustered his will and strength, burning brighter than ever before. The light around him burned as white fire and grew more and more substantial until it became harder than stone. All of his will and determination matched his swelling pride. Regal and invincible he looked.

"Show your strength!" shouted Lucifer to the throngs around him. And each and every angel under his charge mustered all their might to burn bright and hard. A horde of winged creatures hung in the air above while others stood as if braced against a cruel wind. A shimmering sea of wings drew back and upward. Swords of bright white light rose above the wings like a forest of icy towers upon a stormy sea.

Though unspeakable, there, arraigned on the edge of Heaven, was an army of angel kind. They flanked Lucifer's right and left facing the citadel of Elohim. Resolute and unyielding they stood; set and bold. Posed for action, still they thought not of open defiance and warfare with Elohim. But rather, they were confident of their victory which would be won this day in the benevolence of Elohim. For surely, they thought, this day Elohim would bestow his favour on their master for his self determination. And Lucifer was certain above all that the King of Heaven would reward his evolution to equality and grant his secession.

Now, Lucifer knew that all was in the light of Elohim and no thoughts or words spoken this day were hidden. But Lucifer also regarded Michael as rash beyond reason and unable to grasp the deep things of Lucifer's higher mind. And Lucifer commanded Gia with but a motion and a thought to lead out his host and hinder Michael while all awaited the acceptable judgment of Elohim. But Gia was not to the task for Michael came upon them like a violent wind of fire and force.

And before Gia would rise fully to meet Michael, the force before him spun him to the side. The angels around Lucifer pulled back at the sight of such violence. For never had they known such a thing in Heaven.

Fearful was the sight of Michael who hovered as a giant among angels. In golden armor of light, Michael and his legions burst upon Gia and the fallen army of angels. But Lucifer rose to meet Michael in the air with a cry for all to aid him. But at the light of Heaven's blazing guardian, the host behind Lucifer grew uncertain and timid.

Lucifer with his Generals at his heals gathered all his strength and a force of impenetrable light surrounded him as he collided with Michael. Michael was pushed back and his progress halted for a time. And for a moment his strength was drained. But Michael rose as a mountain of light multiplying in size and girth. And the light that was sent forth from him was white hot and hard like metal. Like a sword of light with a thousand blades, Michael assaulted Lucifer and threw him down. Now for the first time, fear entered the heart of Lucifer for he in no way imagined such resistance and strength from Michael.

Michael stood above Lucifer and held him to the ground with the force and light that came from him. All around the two battling princes, angels hewed and slashed - angels striking angels. Like ten thousand blinding star bursts, swords of light clashed and thunderous echoes filled all of Heaven.

Now angels are not as mankind who are wounded and bleed and lose life in the wounding. But angels can be drained of power and light and strength. And for a time, they can be fallen in battle and held captive by their weakness and subdued by greater strength.

As Lucifer lay beneath the foot of Michael, humiliation came over him. All eyes were cast in his direction. The angels who stood with Lucifer were now darting here and there in confusion and chaos, for the battle was all but lost to them. Most were subdued by the greater power of Michael's company. Fearful and frantic, there was no place to retreat as the great swarm of warrior angels hovered above Lucifer's host. A great furor of sound and movement finally slowed and another sound like a distant rumbling thunder, low and sad filled the air.

Lucifer tried once more to free himself from Michael's grip mustering all his strength and power, but angels swarmed to Lucifer and aided Michael's restraint of the fallen Archangel.

And as the gust and surge of Lucifer subsided, all grew silent except for a distant growing moan; somber and cheerless. Whimpers and sobs could be heard as Lucifer hung his head in defeat. The iron grip of Michael became of less concern to

Lucifer, for the low droning noise in the distance grew louder and louder until it became the greatest discomfort to Lucifer. And though he wished now for freedom and hoped that Elohim would come and tear away his oppressor, he longed more for the ceasing of that horrific sound that so distressed him and haunted him to the core. All could see that Heaven had changed and was not as it was. It was murky and dimmer than before. And in every heart there was a sense of gloom never imagined.

As silence fell, a bright light approached the embattled horde and their assailants. It was Gabriel who came, but his appearance was different and though he in diminished form resembled the form of Elohim, he now was brighter and more commanding than ever seen, not unlike Elohim himself but lesser in all respects.

He came and hung above Lucifer for a while before speaking, and in his voice was a sadness. "What have you done Lucifer most privileged of Heaven? What have you done? Do you hear the sound of Elohim who even now weeps from his throne at your madness and evil? For you have this day rebelled against his love and wounded his heart. This day, your heartless betrayal has broken all and everything beyond mending."

Lucifer, his arrogance still peaked shouted "Release me!" to Michael. "I shall see Elohim who is my judge, not you."

Gabriel roared with a thunderous voice that shook the ground on which Lucifer laid. "Silence, you destroyer of dreams, you forger of lies, for I speak for Elohim. My voice is his. My eyes see for him. And my ears will bear the burden of your defense. You shall indeed stand before his throne and see the fruit of your treachery in the torment of his heart. But for now, do not further fuel the anger of one in sorrow. For you have brought to Heaven a suffering that will for a season bow every head and slow every heart. For now, Elohim's tears will flow, but in the turning of Heaven's day will you give account of yourself."

"I am misread," said Lucifer. "Will he not hear my petition? For villains have assailed his great Prince and for no other reason than pride and jealousy. I have a just claim. And he shall see there is no malice in me, but I fear malice undeserved has come upon me."

"Lucifer." Gabriel's tone softened and anger was no longer in his eyes or voice.

"Do you not see your error? For you have returned to the imaginations of which you so eagerly repented. Why was your repentance so false? For now to your imaginations you have gathered strong desires more than before. And now beyond all hope have you sought with all your will to make it so. Your thoughts are contrary to all the goodness and kind intentions of Elohim. Your desires are not of love but the very opposite of love. They are self serving to the loss and harm of all. And your will opposes the will of Elohim whose heart can and will ever only choose the highest for all. While he values you, you in turn depreciate him in your heart. While he honors you and always has, you dishonor him. Though he gives without limit, you would take without regard for the giver. While he loves you with all his heart, all your heart rejects him. When he has made you by love and for love, why have you abandoned love and reason? While all of Heaven was yours and his heart was ever for you, why have you listened to the false council of your own heart?"

Lucifer could not hear the intent of Gabriel's words and repeated his demand. "Release me now!"

Michael looked to Gabriel and in silent agreement Michael took the bonds off of his captive. Anger grew in Lucifer who felt betrayed and mistreated by these lesser angels.

"Elohim," he yelled. "Why do you disregard me?"

Lucifer tried to pass Gabriel and fly to the citadel of Elohim. Michael in a flash stood before him and halted him in his tracks. Lucifer ventured not to defy Michael again and shook with anger.

"Vile creature." said Lucifer "Do you not know who I am? Is this your love and devotion to a brother that you would bar me from justice before the throne of Elohim?"

"Lucifer," said Gabriel "do you forget Elohim? For he is here as near to you as your own skin. He hears your very thoughts and sees all without limit. There is no need to stand before his throne. For now he will in sorrow wait for a time and season to address your every claim. But no thing can escape him and no words can change the outcome of this dreadful hour. His mercy is great but there can be no mercy for a heart that refuses to bend and alter its course. For he can do all things and all good for any with a willing heart; but very little with a heart that is hardened and unwilling such as yours."

"Mercy!" cried Lucifer toward the Citadel.

Gabriel drew close, within a breath of Lucifer, and looked into his eyes which could not look back.

"Did you not taste once of his mercy?" asked Gabriel. "And though you struck him to the heart with vile offense, still he sought the highest and best for you. Did he not pardon your every whim and foul fantasy that injured him so? And in his mercy was your heart not rendered soft again? And what now has his mercy birthed in you? Are you now willing to be what you should always be, a good and faithful friend and servant? No! For these you no longer desire or seek. And now, mercy will have no effect on such a heart but only increase your rebellion. For mercy should look like weakness to you now. He is not weak and will not step aside to see you destroy all of Heaven and Earth with your false thoughts, your selfish desires and the malice of your will. He and all of Heaven will resist you.

Your eye is fixed on the path you have chosen and though he would sway you otherwise and draw you once more into his embrace with joy, you will not change your mind. For you have seen all of him and have stood for ages before his throne and tasted of every kindness. You have known the fullness of him in so much as your form could hold. You have known the heights of limitless joy and peace and walked in unquenchable love. And still you turn away.

What more is there for Elohim to show you or give you or bestow upon you that you have not already seen and felt and tasted? Can he show you more love or more kindness to sway your mind back to its former satisfaction? No, there is no truth or light that you have not known that could now correct your path. You have rejected all that you can be given. So what then is your end but to direct your thoughts and desires and will to that which is not Elohim. You have and will pursue that which has no profit for you or delight for Elohim. There is no hand to catch your fall and this is your pleasure."

"What evil is in this place?" said Lucifer. "Who would come against me with such violence? Surely not Elohim. For I am his creation and his perfect work. I think some trickery has kept your treason in secret. Does the all powerful Elohim equip himself for battle with creatures as insignificant as these?"

Looking to Michael, Lucifer continued "Do you by some foul device keep me from the sympathy and support of Elohim?"

Michael approached Lucifer until breath could be felt and in a firm but strangely gentle voice he spoke. Lucifer's eyes strayed from Michael's as he struggled to look into his bright and burning gaze.

"Lucifer," said Michael, "do you believe that Elohim has need of what little strength I possess or the words and wisdom of Gabriel? Creation this day contends with creation. For today, your creator has no desire to lift his hand in conflict. He will not quarrel with you. This day is a day for grief and suffering, for he still loves the Lucifer that is in his heart. And the treachery of this day slices deep and causes sorrow beyond measure. So here and now, we do his bidding though he has no need of it.

Surely, you know that there can never be a true battle in Heaven for there is no striving against his will in this place. There is no contest between creation and creator. For should he wish to do so, he could slay you with less than a thought. With half a breath could all life cease and the foundations of Heaven and Earth crumble to dust and less. This small strength and blow is just enough to quell your rebellious stride and cool your fevered heart, no more and no less. None can wage war against Elohim. There is no undecided battle and no chance of resistance. Your warfare is a feather thrown against the gale. And though his great love for you has left him with a heavy heart this day, he is indeed a tempest and all consuming fire. Be sure of this when next you stand before him."

Lucifer seemed unaffected by Michael's words and called back to his host; "Come to my aid and open a way for me to the citadel."

Lucifer's defeated army stirred and moved. Some tried in vain to reach Lucifer, most cowered. With fruitless effort, all resolution failed and all fell into an unhappy submission. Sobbing soon became wailing and groaning as they could not move against the mighty angels of Michael's command.

Gabriel spoke once again. "Now, Lucifer I speak for Elohim. My words are his words. Do you contend with me? Will you strive against me? Now I shall show you your end."

All of Heaven darkened and grew black as if a cloud of despair and anger blocked out the sun. But there was no sun to give Heaven light. All light came from Elohim. And Lucifer froze as if a great terror gripped his heart.

From his host came desperate cries; "Mercy! Mercy! Elohim is upon us!"

11

The Far Exile

From the Citadel of Elohim came a mighty, rushing wind and the Spirit of Elohim encircled Lucifer and his host. As if caught in an unseen net, they were dragged through the sky of Heaven to the hall of the King. Pushed and crowded together in a mass of angel flesh, they hung suspended over the Crystal Lake. Heaving and squirming, they were trapped beyond all hope. In fear they tried to cry out but every voice and sound from the captives was silenced. Curses and screams and cries came not from their open, gaping mouths. In anguish did they try but no sound could they make. Elohim by his own hand had fastened them together in an unseen prison, towing them against there wills and futile struggle before the throne. This was what Lucifer had desired and demanded, but now held and bound by the wrath of Elohim, Lucifer had great misgivings and wished for the farthest end of Heaven.

The fire that burned on and above the throne of Elohim burned brighter in the midst of a darkened Heaven. The wind of the Spirit gathered around the throne and the rushing noise subsided.

"Lucifer, what do you seek from me?" came a voice from the midst of the fire. "For you were not content to allow my sorrow room and place. To my sorrow you would add. Now, your demand is met. But you shall wish that today was a day for sorrow and not demanding. What is it that you seek?"

Lucifer was unleashed from the mob and like a limp rag was drawn and held aloft before the throne. He shook with fear as he kept his head bowed. The bluster of pride earlier displayed was all but diminished. He felt now humiliation and anger.

"I seek justice, oh King of Heaven!" cried Lucifer.

"Do you not seek mercy?" asked Elohim.

"I have no need of mercy," said Lucifer. "And to confess the need of it would encourage this great injustice. For is not mercy for the wrongdoer but justice is for the wronged?"

"Where have you been wronged and from whom does your affliction come?" asked Elohim. Lucifer was careful with his answer. "I am and always have been your servant," he said "but this day I have been overthrown by those who falsely claim to be so. For there is in your realm a secret plot to remove me from my position and my due reward. This day, Heaven's guardians struck me down without cause or remorse and in doing so have blamed your hand."

Elohim spoke from the throne; "You know well this was indeed my hand, so now do you try to deceive me? Do you cry injustice and plead ignorance to all that has come upon you?"

"Are you now the accuser of your brethren even though your very future is in peril? It is you Lucifer who stand accused and condemned for such acts as never have been seen or imagined in Heaven from the beginning till now. You are right in that you have no need for mercy. For mercy would I gladly extend if mercy could change your heart. But this day you shall have justice and so shall all of Heaven.

Now speak your mind and disclose your intentions without falsehood or fraud. For I shall silence your voice forever should you hide your true ambitions."

Lucifer spoke slowly at first; "It was not in this way bound and dragged that I desired to present to you my petition. But now I am cornered and trapped against my intentions. I have therefore little recourse but to disclose my rightful claim to all. Though the manner in which I do so is unworthy of such a good and rightful claim. Whether Prince or prisoner, the claim is just.

You, King of Heaven have given me life but to this I was not a part. Still grateful, I have lived to the fullness of your intentions and my design. And now I see that I am grown beyond your intentions. To this you deserve proper praise and honor. For how great a being have you begun that I now have completed. And still in my future there is more that I can be, all to your glory and honor.

I am a creature of life and by creating me you have given me rights to my own life and my own course. So do I now need consent to grow and become what I am and most certainly will be? I desire nothing less than to be as my creator and share with him the wonder of this creation."

Lucifer's voice became more bold as anger filled his heart. "Now, this day I see that you are not for me and I see that Elohim is less than all he has spoken. For "love" he says but I am thrown down and humiliated and bound. Is this love? Free I am made, but when my freedom exceeds his want then freedom is no longer mine.

And now shall I appeal to Elohim to be true to himself and grant me all that is in my heart. For that which is in my heart is surely no threat to Elohim.

Now I see clearly that my purposes do not harmonize with the rule of Elohim in this place. So then, if discontented with me here in this place, is it so great a thing to give to me a realm of my own? Is there not happy accord that Heaven should be without me? But as we cannot come to understanding in this place, should not Elohim create a place and realm, for his own satisfaction, where I am free to do all that is good to do. And wise as Elohim is, surely he should know that I will strive to be a good and gracious King of my own realm. And if Elohim never comes to satisfaction with me then should he not think of my realm as a satisfactory exile that serves us both equally?

Now, I have seen by my own eyes how worlds come at Elohim's summons. The world of man below though fragile and soft and temporal would indeed make me an acceptable home. And Elohim can rest in peace knowing that I would be a benevolent King of such a realm. And if this realm is not for the offering then should Elohim not create another for my exile and freedom and all that I have a rightful claim to? Here now is a solution where there is no victim, no injustice and no indictment of the innocent. All is fair and agreeable and profitable."

Lucifer was lowered to the ground and stood on his own in front of the fire. For the first time Lucifer felt heat from that fire. So strong was the heat that Lucifer tried to step back and away from it. But though standing on the ground, he was not free to move.

The voice from the fire spoke yet again; "Your name is no longer Lucifer, the shining one. This day you have opposed your maker and desired beyond all reason that which would destroy the very foundations of Heaven and Earth and all creation. This day, fault of your own making has been found in you. For you have chosen a path of deception. For never before was there any false notion in Heaven pursued by the heart.

You have called that which is right, wrong and that which is wrong, right. You have birthed a lie; the first lie. And you now are the father of lies and the victim of your own devices. You have believed, against all hope, the very lies you forged. You have called darkness, light and light, darkness. Your vision is distorted. Your thoughts are twisted. Your reason is unreasonable. Reality, truth and sanity you have left at the foot of the door and have closed it behind you for all time. You have seen that which is not, and called it true and right. Your imagination envisions an image of Elohim that is less than I am. Your distorted vision is all you see. Lies keep you from seeing what is. In your heart lies a picture of Elohim; false and crooked and corrupt. And you would spread these falsehoods and fantasies until all of Heaven sees as you see. You would blind all eyes and twist every heart by the lies that now rule your heart.

You are no longer Lucifer, for you are the adversary of Elohim and of Heaven and of all truth and life. You are Satanas. Your poison is in your tongue and you shall in no way repent of the false lies and false visions your heart has conjured."

Lucifer tried to speak but could utter no words. Elohim knowing his heart continued;

"There is no sound defense in you and no words worth hearing but more lies do you conjure to bring about a deceptive end. Still, my heart is that you would see your folly and know the truth of who I am and see and know my great love and heart that has always been for you. But your lies are a gate slammed in the face of all reason and revelation. Even as I speak of my love and my sorrow over the loss of my son this day, does your heart imagine ill will in me. I have no words to show you what you have already dismissed.

And so it is to your end that I shall send you. But first, you shall sojourn in this new realm that you desire more than the love of Elohim. You shall be witness of my true love and kind heart for my children, and they shall rule over you and keep you at bay until such a time that you shall inherit your kingdom. But the realm you inherit is a terror to those who love life. You are Satanas. You are the adversary of all. Look now upon your fate and your chosen destiny."

As Elohim finished his pronouncement, a wind in Heaven began to blow from every direction toward the heart of Heaven and the Lake before the throne. As the winds converged, a funnel formed swirling above the great sea of crystal. As it spun, ever increasing in size and speed, all the darkness that lay heavy in Heaven was caught up in its grasp until a long dark, black whirlwind swayed and drifted angrily about the face of the Lake. The wind in the tempest was loud and terrifying to all who hung imprisoned above its open, gaping mouth.

Satanas' dangling hordes screamed and cried out for fear they would be swallowed up into the vortex. They cried out for help first to their master, and when none came to free them, they cried out to Elohim for mercy. But they were not that day rescued from their fate. For into the mouth of the violent storm they were sucked and a blur of angel flesh and darkness spun in a chaotic ballet of horror and fear. Cursing could be heard in echoes throughout Heaven.

Then the thundering whirlwind descended into the Lake and into the world of man and yet another dimension and new world was born. The funnel of blackness and wind became a shaft leading to a dark and loathsome place somewhere in the bowels of man's realm on a far plane in the universe of man. But the mouth of the funnel was closer to man's own world. Now this dark place was not of the same substance of the world below and did not touch or hinder the world of man. Like a world within a world, it was there but further away than any could travel. Unseen by human eyes and only for a season could angels know of its place in man's world.

All the darkness left Heaven as it was gathered and dragged into the funnel. And slowly the world that held captive a host of fallen became dim and distant and less visible. The terrible uproar slowly diminished for sound and light were swallowed up in the blackness of that place. Only the distant sound of weeping and gnashing of teeth could be heard for a time. And so it became a far-flung place; remote and forsaken.

Now Elohim looked to Satanas and said, "This too is your fate. A realm you shall have."

And Elohim opened Satanas' mouth and gave him power once again to speak.

"Elohim!" cried Satanas. "What treachery and cruelty is this? Do you now prove my rash appraisal of your character and heart. For where is your love in this act and loathsome exile to such a torment? You do yourself injustice to give so many cause to doubt and question your love and character. Turn now away from this verdict and free those whom you would imprison. You do not deserve, do you, to have all of Heaven challenge your goodness in such a wayward judgment? Come now back to your rightful place of justice and mercy and render to all the love that I know is in your heart."

"And I Satanas know what is in your heart," said Elohim.

"I cannot give you what you desire. Only can I give you what you deserve and what is best for Heaven and Earth below. Though you shall never be agreeable to my end and never accept my purposes and never understand my reasons, still I shall explain myself in this banishment of evil.

You have chosen a path which was never in my heart for you. And I can in no way allow the lies and deception born in your heart to infect those who in innocence still pursue love and truth. In choosing your own path, your heart first must deny me and challenge me. This day in your selfish heart, you devised a perfect realm of your own design for your own happiness, while you tried to deny me of all my happiness. Your will this day, sprung from deception in your heart, is to live apart from me and my love and my will. For I am no longer your King. You have a new King and Lord. His name is Satanas. For this day you are both monarch and subject in your own kingdom. You have chosen to bar me from your life and future. You have removed me from your heart and accused me falsely. Your lies have convinced you that I am less than you have known and loved. And now your heart has no room for me. You have made me your opponent in all and everything.

And still though you would deny me your love and friendship, your service and devotion, your obedience and trust, you would take what I would give. You desire power but I can only offer love and relationship. You desire freedom to do all you will.

But that freedom would hinder all that is good and right and would choose the very opposite of love and value. You would destroy Heaven to make for yourself a kingdom and then you seek my approval and aid to do so.

I can give you none of these things you desire because I love and am true. But I give you what I can and what you desire in part.

For you do not desire me. This day you have said, 'not Elohim's will but my will - not Elohim's path but the path of my choosing.' And now you long for all that is not Elohim. This you shall have. For I have prepared a place for you in which I am not. In this place, you shall never see me, nor see my love, nor hear my voice. My will is foreign to this place and there my heart cannot be felt or understood. There is, in this dark realm, no revelation or light of Elohim. My spirit will not go to and fro in this place. Neither is the weight of my hand upon you in this realm.

And though you would love all of this if only the beauty and wonder of all my creation were there, this I cannot do. For to hate me and reject me is to hate all that comes from my hand and heart. In this dark place, the light of Elohim does not shine and the creation of my hand is not there. It is empty and void of all that I am. For all my creation is a gift of love from one to another; from Elohim to Elohim; from Father to Son and Spirit and from Elohim to the children below. And no gift of love shall be in your realm - no colour, no light, no growing, living thing, no beauty, no joyful thing. And all that is there has nothing to do with me."

For the first time Satanas cried, not in sad repentance as before but in despair of his fate and future.

Elohim continued and the grief could be heard in his voice. "This is your realm and none shall find a trace of Elohim in this place. And none shall know their purpose and value. This I give you, for you indeed have tasted freedom as none other. And with your freedom and your lies and your selfish desires, you have purchased an inheritance for all eternity."

As Satanas wept all of Heaven wept as well. Gabriel looked down at Lucifer and felt helpless. Michael hung his head as he loved his brother but now in his eyes his brother was no more.

"Satanas," said Elohim, "though this be your end, first shall you dwell in the land of the living where my children rule in my stead. And you shall see in them my kind intentions and know the destiny which you have this day rejected. And you shall have no power or force or light as you have in Heaven. You shall be a stranger and wanderer in this land until I send you to your home. And no weapon shall you forge and no harm shall you cause by force or by arms. You shall be an empty vessel of little worth and sore to look upon. Your beauty is forfeit and your life is your own to your eternal regret."

Upon the heals of the last word of Elohim, Michael took hold of Satanas and rose to the heights of Heaven's hall and with a cry of deep pain threw Satanas into the Lake of Crystal and like a bolt of lightening Satanas flashed through the Lake and fell to the Earth below. Like a burning meteor, he flew into the sky above the Earth and as he did his light slowly burned out. And the brilliant flash of light that began his journey ended with a grey and colourless being huddled on the floor of the Earth not far from the garden in which the children of Elohim dwelt.

All of Heaven wept as they gazed into the world beneath the Crystal Lake. And turning again toward the pillar of fire that rose above the throne, weeping turned to wails and all fell prostrate before the throne for none could stand before the broken heart of Elohim, Father, Son and Spirit.

12

A Shadow In The Garden

Now the world of man, of flesh and stone is not the world of spirit and light where Elohim's throne rests. And the fall of Satanas to the Earth below was the final step in his abandonment of reason and love and all things of value; decent and civilized.

Standing to his feet and looking at the frail beauty around him, Satanas pronounced, to himself and to all and any who would witness, his distain for all that was of and from and for Elohim. And so great was his twisted sense of injustice and the weight of his judgment that his heart became engulfed by boundless rage. No pride or arrogance or malice was diminished that day, but all and every part of his being turned to its complete and final defiance of all he once knew. The last residue of reason became insanity. A heart that once held love was now only and always full of hate.

The surpassing beauty of creation for which he once lusted and jealously desired was now hideous to his eyes. As he gazed at the world around him, he longed to both own it and destroy it all. And if ears could hear his heart they would burn at his hateful thoughts.

"This day," spoke his twisted heart, "I am indeed Satanas. Adversary I am called and so shall I be. For that which Elohim loves I shall hate with all that I am. And to all life, I desire death. To all joy, I shall seek its end in misery. To all that is peace, I shall bring warfare and torment. Where hope resides, I will quench it with the fire of despair. I shall hate that which Elohim loves. His beauty is vile to my eyes. And my art and my beauty shall smite his senses and foul all that is precious to him. His pain shall be my pleasure and his grief shall be my delight. And all that he cherishes shall I despise and destroy and murder."

Where the first evil and malice were birthed in the heart Lucifer, they were now his one ambition.

Satanas looked down to the ground around his feet and saw that the beauty of the garden had spread beyond the garden and would flower in time the whole Earth. A sickness welled up inside him for now the colours and textures and designs around him were repulsive to his eyes and dreadful to his heart. In rage, he tore at the plants and flowers and shrubs beneath him. But as he sought mindless destruction of all he saw, life repaired, grew and multiplied around him. The more he assaulted the Earth, the faster was its healing, for far greater was the power of creation than his want to destroy. He sunk low to the ground and hung his head. "There is yet another way to do battle," he said. "And I shall find it."

Adam and Eve grew together as man and wife and were rarely parted. For great was the pleasure they knew in one another. So often did they thank

Elohim for the gift of love and partnership. They were as children in their hearts, but in their play and sport, they grew in wisdom day by day. Their understanding and knowledge of the world around them and of their father and creator increased and multiplied daily.

Everyday, just as the sun settled and a lesser light filled their sky and cool shadows crept across the garden, Elohim would come and walk with them for a while. Together, they talked and laughed and took joy in each others presence. Adam and Eve were unaware of the grief and loss that had come upon Elohim.

Gabriel too would come into the garden and though Heaven was shut to Adam and Eve, some from Heaven were free to move in and out of man's world. Gabriel was the foremost privileged in this respect and he was free to walk beside the children of Elohim. And though he was tutor and counselor, he was friend as well and came not for duty but for pleasure.

One evening after Elohim had departed, Gabriel had wandered into Eden's courtyard. There Adam and Eve sat on the ground before the two trees. Their gaze was fixed on the Tree of Life and were unaware of Gabriel's presence. The fruit on the tree was young and the tree was barely more than a sapling. The fruit of the Tree of the Knowledge of Good and Evil was still there but looked withered and less appealing than the smaller fruit of the Tree of Life. As Gabriel's shadow fell in front of Adam and Eve, they turned with a smile. Gabriel sat beside them and said nothing.

"How long?" asked Eve.

"The time is coming," said Gabriel; "but you cannot hurry your tutelage. You are growing in understanding and your devotion to Elohim is strong, your character is true for one so young. But all has yet to be tested to the point of secure and unfaltering strength. The promise is yours but do not desire it before its time."

"I feel I am now full and complete and ready for all Elohim has for us," said Adam.

"So says every young buck and calf that stands yet on wobbly legs," said Gabriel.

"My legs are sure and strength is in them and in my heart as well," blurted Adam.

Gabriel looked a few meters away and drew Adam and Eve's attention to a small crack in the ground.

"Do you see this rupture here in this hard ground?" asked Gabriel. "What has caused this?"

Adam and Eve looked closer.

"There is a small seedling in its center that has broken through this ground," said Eve.

Adam saw and knew but listened without response.

"Which is the harder and the stronger, the ground or the plant?" asked Gabriel.

Eve smiled for her mind was already to the end of Gabriel's journey and Adam with her but she slowed her pace and played the student to her master.

"Reason and sight would tell me that the ground was the harder for it can bear my full weight while the tender shoot cannot. And I could bruise my heal to stir the ground while the flower will shred at a gentile pull of my hand."

"True," said Gabriel, "and yet the flower had ripped the hard soil with no bruise and no harm and is clearly the victor here."

"It would seem," said Adam.

"The hardness of the ground aids this little plant in its victory." said Gabriel. "One resists the other and the shoot prevails. The flower owes its life and strength to the very ground that would keep it from life. The ground resists and so the shoot struggles and strives. The more it pushes and the more the ground resists the stronger the seedling grows. So too your strength, your faith and your character grows to conquer that which would stand against it. But your strength is not complete. Soon the ground shall split and you shall be ready to taste the air of Heaven."

Gabriel in a comforting gesture reached out his hands and squeezed their shoulders. "Time, my little ones, it is your ally not your foe."

"Grow this garden and let time be your friend and aid you."

Adam looked puzzled. "Are we here to grow this garden?" he asked Gabriel. "Surely Elohim has no need of gardeners."

Gabriel laughed a deep rolling laugh, and turning to the two gently replied. "My little ones, the garden is here to grow you."

Gabriel turned and began to walk away still chuckling. He turned back and almost as an after thought said; "As for you, you will grow an eternal empire."

Adam and Eve grew again in wisdom and understanding that very hour.

The three stood together and began to walk down a path into a stand of trees under a roof of green. This was the most quiet part of the garden where every sound seemed swallowed in the woods.

"Teacher;" said Adam "what of the shadow?"

"The shadow?" asked Gabriel. "Of what do you speak?"

"We have seen it just on the edge of the garden several times," said Eve. "It moves like a breeze but is dark. It seems to swallow the light it touches. Whenever we approach, it disappears. We sense its alarm in our presence as if it feared us. Though I have called to it, it stays at a distance. It obeys not my voice. Where all in the garden does our bidding, this shadow seems not to hear or know or obey."

"And twice now," Adam added "I have been strongly tempted to subdue it and render it compliant but a warning in my heart has told me to let it go."

Gabriel groaned a little and lowered his head "Ummm" moaned Gabriel. "Compliant, oh that it were so."

Gabriel motioned for them to come very close and in the tongues of angels he spoke to them.

"Elohim," said Gabriel, "has seen fit to release under your dominion a powerless malice which would contend with you but is impotent and lacks all but the will to do so. This is one who once stood before Elohim and gave allegiance and love and honor, but who now regrets all and repents of love and goodness and rightness."

Adam and Eve were speechless.

"He was once a King and Prince of angels, a Lord of Elohim's realm. He was as well a brother and friend to me. But there was a foul rebellion that spawned evil and great grief. It was he who stood opposed to all that was good and perfect. He birthed selfishness in a land of love. He took and would not give. He dreamed and lied and lusted for power and stood against truth. He wounded all and sank a dark arrow of grief into Elohim's heart. And still now in Heaven every tongue tastes the bite of his bitterness."

"Why is he here?" asked Eve. "And what has he to do with us? Shall this shadow contend with us and lurk throughout our realm?"

"Of this, we have already spoken," said Gabriel. "For he too is the ground which shall break before your strength and his very presence shall give you cause to pursue Elohim with all your heart. He unwittingly contributes to your devotion. For this shadow is a vision of the very opposite of love. To see him is to hate his end, and to hate that end is to choose life forever and always."

Adam and Eve remembered the tender shoot and the crack in the ground.

Adam asked, "Will he strengthen us and mature us and aid us in our destiny? Can evil benefit good?"

"Not as such," said Gabriel. "His evil is of no value. He is but a warning and example of that which has no place or pleasure in Elohim.

When a tree falls, who would stand to catch it. All who have wisdom would move out of its way to save injury. And if one is caught in its fall, those who witness the pain and harm shall flee a falling tree with greater zeal. He is a fire that burns on your heals to speed you on your way. For you are running a race toward the ultimate prize. And as you run, should you look back over your shoulder to see him lurking there, his dreadful appearance and repulsive state shall speed your progress and clear your vision and ripen your determination to run and win.

Elohim would say to you; 'this is not your end. Do not go down the path that leads to such destruction. Always choose life. For this shadow though it moves and thinks and hates is walking death.'"

Adam turned to look around perhaps wondering if he would see the shadow even now as they spoke. But there was only the silence of the dense woods.

"Elohim's foe is my foe," said Adam. "Should I muster my strength and that of all creation and pursue this creature? Should I route him and cast him out of this our realm? For has not Elohim declared that we and all our children shall rule over every living, breathing, moving creature in this our domain?"

"The children of Elohim need not contend with this wretched creature," declared Gabriel. "For he is no foe except in his own mind. His judgment is pronounced and his destiny is all but secured and final. Only time is the issue. And the time he has depends on you my friends. Give him room and room he shall take. Give him opportunity and he shall surely run to it. Deny him all and he shall have none. This is your realm to rule and so rule this shadow not with force or will but with purity of devotion and unwavering loyalty to your Lord and King. You are the children of Elohim; let no thing dissuade you."

Now Satanas though living in the world of flesh and stone, of water and air was of angel kind and needed no thing on the Earth. His body was of spirit and not flesh. While he wandered the world to its far corners, he most often stayed close to the garden in order to spy on the children of Elohim. And how he hated them for no reason other than the love of Elohim and the joy they brought him.

Though seen as shadow by human eyes, his substance was far more. And this enemy of all life quickly learned his capacities within the realm of man. Though the light of Elohim was gone from him, he could for a short while manifest a light of his own making; much like the lesser light found in the realm of man to which he was now exiled. He could for a time hover and fly and travel at great speeds across the Earth but not to his full ambition. His being could move in and through the material of this world. No wall could bar him and he could pass freely through all objects. Still with direction of his will he could touch and hold all things and could move rock and tree and plant with limited power and force.

But he could destroy nothing, for there was a power in creation that came from Elohim. And man ruled that power to Satanas' misery. The light of Elohim was in Adam and Eve and was fearful to Satanas. And so he kept his watch on the children of Elohim but maintained his distance and ventured never too close to them. For their very words were master over him.

13

The Fall

Now Satanas discovered that he could move within and through the creatures in the Earth, many of which were weak in mind driven by instinct. And clothing himself with their bodies, he learned to control those feeble minds. This was of little value to him for no harm could he do and only for short times could he withstand their instinctive resistance. Still it became sport to him. And clothed in the flesh of beasts, Satanas ventured ever closer to the garden and deeper into the heart of man's abode.

And of all the creatures on the Earth, there was one of greater mind and less instinct. It was as well beautiful to Adam and Eve. Like all things of beauty, it was loathsome to Satanas. And Satanas took upon himself a challenge to rule the mind of this beast and walk in its body.

One day, Satanas took hold of the beast called the prancer, for it rose up high in the air and moved from side to side as it moved. It was indeed the most graceful of all creatures. Its colours too were rich, being covered with jewel-like scales. Its fragrance was as the perfume of flowers. And its song was sweet to hear.

After wrestling long into the day, the beast succumbed and gave way for a time to Satanas' will.

"I tire, take what is not yours and do as you wish," thought the beast.

And Satanas walked in the body of the prancer. Coming to the edge of the garden, Satanas did not see or sense Adam and Eve and venturing ever deeper, he came upon the clearing in the center of the garden.

Now Satanas in his secret surveillance had discovered over time the intention and purpose of the two trees in the middle of the garden but now saw them for the first time. And how he longed to see the children of Elohim fall from their place of honor and fortune in the eyes of Elohim. And it seemed to him that only the Tree of the Knowledge of Good and Evil could advance his cause.

Adam and Eve were once again in the courtyard measuring the trees and the fruit of the two trees. And even now the fruit of the Tree of the Knowledge of Good and Evil was failing. Its leaves were diminished and its fruit less hearty than ever before.
Out of the corner of his eye, Adam saw the shape of the prancer just beyond the first row of trees hiding in the shadows. He tapped Eve on the arm to show her the sight.

"I have never seen such a one so deep in the garden before," said Eve.

Adam raised his voice and bid the creature to draw close.

Satanas was caught before he could bolt away as he had so many times before. He moved reluctantly toward them in compliance for now even he could not refuse the rule of the children of Elohim. And knowing he would be discovered, he mustered all his strength and burned bright a false light in his being that shone through the flesh of the creature. And the beauty of the beast seemed greater than ever before. In mock confidence, he strode with pride and arrogance toward the children of light and the Kings of the Earth as if he belonged there in this place.

"And what is this?" said Eve. "Have I not seen you and played with you in the plains beyond the woods? Still you are not the same creature, are you?"

"I am not," said Satanas.

"I know who you are," said Adam; "for I see with my eyes a shadow across this beast. And shadow you are indeed who hides in unlikely places."

"I am not hiding!" said Satanas. "For I have no need to do so. For this beast whom you love has given me that which is most precious to him. He knows I am true indeed and gifts are for friends. But how is it that you call me shadow. Who has instructed you in the knowledge of one such as me?"

Adam walked close to the beast and examined him. "You are who you are and all is known to us," said Adam. "Depart now this place and silence your voice before us."

"Are you not the Kings of the Earth?" asked Satanas. "And am I not under your authority? Surely you can abide me for a time without hindrance or peril. Am I a threat to the children of Elohim?"

"No threat," said Eve. "We abide what we will at our pleasure not yours. We know who you are."

"With great respect and honor, I think not," said Satanas. "Though truly you know what you have been told. Is there room in you to see for yourselves if those words describe what your eyes see? Can you not measure me yourselves? Such is the role of Kings and judges."

Adam grew impatient but Eve looked over to Adam and spirit to spirit spoke out of Satanas' hearing;

"Slow my husband," she said to Adam "wait, watch and query. We two have no need for rash action. We are safe from beast and shadow. And in this foul beast, we shall see with our eyes what we have only heard with our ears and prove Gabriel and Elohim true."

"If you can bear me," said Satanas; "I will tell you who I am. For I was once as you, a child and Prince in a realm that appeared the perfection of love and honor and justice. And now, I am cast down, and in sorrow, will bear an injustice to which I have no witnesses. For power rules where power wants, but true justice rules and aids both powerful and powerless. If power is my accuser to whom can I turn for justice?"

"You have justice from he who is both powerful and just. And we are done with you." said Eve.

"Then, I am done altogether," sighed Satanas. "For even the ears of Kings will not hear my petition. Will none stand for justice or at the very least with pity give justice a voice? If I am guilty then my end is assured, for sentence is passed and pronounced before ever there was a trial to test my case. And if I am innocent, are there none who would try me? Will you in mercy not hear me? For what harm can I do? If I be right or wrong still I am ruined. Ask me any question and you shall hear me and judge and only promise me this, that I may ask you but one question to prove my claim."

Adam was now silent and was resigned to remain so. If Eve would hear this creature then Adam would restrain himself and stand with his wife.

"What then is your crime?" asked Eve.

"I uncovered a hidden truth too hard for all of Heaven. It was no crime at all," said Satanas.

"What truth?" asked Eve.

"I have seen behind the veil and lifted the mask behind which Elohim hides. For he is not who he says he is."

Eve was outraged and her heart stung at the very thought that Elohim could be false. "No more questions. You have indeed fallen," said Eve.

"My queen," petitioned Satanas. "What of the question you promised me. Surely, you will honor my request and your promise."

"Speak your mind now for the last time," broke in Adam. Now, both he and Eve wanted this to end.

"Have you measured Elohim's words as you have measured mine?" asked Satanas. "Is it true; has Elohim said 'you shall not eat from any of the trees in the garden?' Does he deny you so much?"

Eve indignant at the accusation defended Elohim. "This is not so, we can indeed eat from any tree in this garden, but for the tree you see before you. Of this tree, he has said "You shall not eat from it nor touch it, nor desire it. For the day that you eat from the Tree of the Knowledge of Good and Evil, you shall surely die."

Satanas looked at the tree and smiled and looking back to Adam and Eve with a slight laugh in his voice said; "So he has denied you. Of this I was certain. Truthfully my Lords, you will not die! Is this the command of a father to a child? For what father could deny knowledge to his children? You suppose, as did I, a good intention and innocent purpose in this restriction. But love does not deny such knowledge. There is an unseen purpose that I have seen and for which I suffer.

Oh that I had not seen and known the truth. For happy would I be in bliss and ignorance in the false proclamations of Elohim. For which is better; truth and misery or deception and contentment?

He denies you, in this we are agreed, but for what purpose? For Elohim knows that in the day you eat from this tree, you will become as he is. And how he would keep you from such heights. He would have no equals or peers. Be not deceived. This is the tree that shall bring you to your fullness, not the other. The other called 'life' will truly give you power and freedom and an eternal body of limitless dimensions, yes. But first you must partake of this almost dead tree. The one before the other or none you shall have. For if this tree dies then the other will too be denied and taken from this place. You shall have neither; no knowledge befitting the children of Elohim, and then no power and freedom with which to yield such knowledge. Both shall be lost to you. But trust in my words and trust also your heart, this one here clinging to life will give you knowledge. And he does not want you to know and be all that you can be. And without knowledge and power and freedom, he will have fashioned for himself a fettered slave in a kingly cage. Can you not see that he is keeping you from rising to your full potential?"

Satanas could see the questions and doubts rising in both Adam and Eve's minds. A strong voice within Eve responded, "How could Elohim have such questionable motives for all his great acts and service? Have we not tasted of his goodness?"

Satanas responded to the unasked question. "Why, you might wonder, would Elohim provide so well and nurture you with all he has given if the end is less than honorable? A wooden bowl, a walking stick, a stool to sit upon, all begin their life as trees nurtured and encouraged to grow until felled by hands to serve such hands at the heart's whim. The ripest fruit is robbed of life to feed another. So you are grown and harvested to serve the desire of another. You can escape such an end, if you grasp what has been denied to you. But if you wait too long, you shall be little more than a tool in the belt of a craftsman who builds his own house with the life of another."

Satanas looked for a favourable response and could see the struggle in both minds before him.

"And is this love and friendship?" he continued. "Does he care for you or manipulate you to his own end? There is nothing of harm in this tree. So bright does Elohim shine in your eyes and so dark will you be all your days. You are bound by deceptive words and kept as a prisoner here in this place that so appeals to you, but keeps you from all you should be.

Is this the heart of a father or a tyrant? And if you desire proof than look to me. Look at my state and all I am. Oh that you could have seen what was stolen from me. And if you continue to walk blindly down a lesser path, this too is your destiny.

You have a realm given to you and you are Kings indeed and are free to do what I could not. You can steer your destiny in that good direction that he would keep from you. Can you trust one who would hinder you so? I tell you as one who has little to gain and nothing to lose. He is not who he says he is! And your blind trust fuels his power and denies your fulfillment. This tree is indeed your ally until it dies and all hope shall be lost to you as is his will."

Adam remained silent and spoke not his mind. The unity between he and his bride would not be challenged and so he sat in wait and passively, quietly condoned all that followed.

Eve turned to her silent husband and looked for guidance but none was there. In her eyes, she pleaded with Adam for some assurance. An emptiness she had never known devoured her. Still she sought refuge in Adam. Eve felt lost and desperately off course. Every word of the prancer and the shadow within made such sense to her. She began to lose sight of Elohim in her mind. The vision of him became obscured and distant. Eve forgot Elohim and forgot his love and his heart. She could no longer even remember the sound of his voice.

A relentless torrent of questions battered her mind and unearthed the deepest suspicions. She wondered and muttered under her breath. Was she thinking these thoughts or somehow hearing the mind of the shadow? She looked up at the beast before her. The shadow was still there.

"Did he speak?" she wondered. "Are these my thoughts or is this his voice I hear?"

"What would you say?" yelled Eve to the prancer.

"Princess of the Earth, I have spoken enough and have no more words to win your heart. I only await your wisdom. For you need not hear more. You see with your own mind clearly what is true. Above all, trust yourself as I trust you with my very life."

The creature stopped speaking but still the questions assaulted Eve. Whether hers or not, they were unyielding and bitter.

"And what of Elohim?" thought Eve. "Were all his heavenly dreams and visions only tales and stories told to children's naive hearts? Was this little more than gullible game and sport? And were all these tales and stories naught but smoke and sparks now blown and scattered by a sober wind of reason? And what of these intoxicating visions of splendor and delight found here in this garden? Were they but conjured illusions? Was this real and true or a thin deception to keep us dim and docile?"

Eve searched still the heart of Adam for an anchor to halt her drift, a compass to guide her home, a gentle wind to blow her to safe harbors. But Adam hung his head and said nothing and gave no hope, no correction and no aid. For Adam too had given way and surrendered to the emptiness of doubt. No rescue would come from Adam.

Standing near as ever to her husband, she felt alone and abandoned to her doubts and fears. For if Elohim was not for her then all was lost. Hope slipped away. She felt as if she had awoken from a dream only to be plunged into the terror of the darkest nightmare. Where was Adam? Who was this stranger beside her?

"Adam must know!" she thought.

Maybe he had always known. Surely he would turn this tide and smote this beast if his words were indeed false. Adam's silence fed Eve's doubt. Doubt became turmoil and anguish. And her heart sought hope from one who had already lost his own.
Eve turned now to the tree and looked at the fruit that hung from its withering branches.

She turned to Satanas and felt anger but at what she knew not.

"Is this the tree I thought it was? Is this not fruit for the eating?" Eve asked.

"Adam," she said "look to this creature before us, loathsome and rejected. Is this his doing or that of another? Is he a picture of our fate?"

She looked over to the fruit on the tree and asked, "Could true love deny us?"

Eve walked around the tree without taking her eyes off of it.

"And we are surely denied," whispered Eve to herself.

"Is Elohim true or do we dangle from unseen strings? I see a tree with fruit fit for eating. And if the eating is for our knowledge and freedom then why is it not for us? If we are Kings indeed then this can only be for our benefit and not against us. If this tree is good for eating as well as knowledge, then what of all that we have been told?"

Eve reached out and plucked a fruit from the tree. And holding it in her hands, she laughed a nervous laugh, as if caught in a hoax.

"Have I been blinded?" she scoffed. "This fruit is not life and death. How foolish could we be to see only what we were told to see."

She looked to Adam for an approving glance. Adam sat in silence.

"Eve must be right," he thought and no words he heard did he oppose.

Eve bit into the fruit and passed it to Adam who did the same.

And turning to the beast before her, she smiled and said "there is no death here. It is only fruit." She dropped the fruit to the ground.

Now, before Eve and Adam who was with her could ever eat from the tree, they had to believe the lies offered to them by the prancing serpent. In sweet words, Satanas challenged Elohim and painted a picture as vile and self-serving as his own heart. In his discourse, he tore down the image of Elohim that held the affection and trust of Adam and Eve. And in that good image they once sought refuge and found joy and life. But the words of Satanas fueled their imaginations until a new and questionable image was fashioned in their hearts by the master and father of lies.

Their eyes were opened to see what was not there at all; to see and imagine a false and terrible picture, far from the true image of Elohim. But false as that image was, it became real to them and a challenge rose in their hearts toward Elohim. The lie took hold of them and all their trust for King and Father was withdrawn. All affection took flight. The unthinkable shook Heaven and Earth as the children of Elohim, heirs of the Kingdom of light and love, believed a lie. The children of Elohim believed a lie and the liar who fashioned them.

And the lie possessed them and became to them as truth. And no words could now rebuild what was broken and no thought was so strong as to challenge the lie now anchored in their heart concerning Elohim.

Their blind hearts and smitten minds conjured a hideous picture of their maker. Elohim could no longer be the center of their affections.

In their hearts, they said, "Elohim is not who he says he is and we cannot believe him. For where is love in such a heart and where is truth in one like Elohim? And does he not claim all for himself but give none to us? Who is this King of Heaven but false and terrible? And now shall he rule us with his will and not his heart? No! We shall not be ruled by such as he."

And there in this gentle garden, that knew only love and play and innocence, Adam and Eve took back what was always surrendered to Elohim. They reclaimed for themselves all their imagined rights and all their own desires. And they said, "We shall be our own masters and none, even Elohim, shall steer our course. We shall reign and rule the lives we own and this realm we have been given."

Satanas smiled.

14

The Broken Heart Of The King

Gabriel hovered above the garden watching and hearing everything. Michael stood watch at his side. Michael would have once again silenced Satanas' voice and subdued him with all his strength, but for the Spirit of Elohim who forbid this or any intervention. Michael flew to and fro, angry and forlorn. Gabriel wept not believing his eyes and ears. He too was restrained from action. Bolting out of the garden Gabriel sped with all his might back to the Citadel of Elohim. But Michael would not suspend his vigilance. He hovered there waiting and hoping for the call of Elohim to put a final end to this treachery.

In rapid flight like a blazing star, Gabriel broke through Heaven's gate rocketing through the Crystal Lake to the full height of the Citadel. Such was the fury of his flight that a fountain of crystal blue water rose around him pursuing him to the peak of Heaven's great hall. He halted his flight abruptly in shock at the sight before him. The water fell like heavy rain from the roof of the Citadel.

All of Heaven was gathered there before Elohim. Angels flew in all direction, frenzied and distraught. For all eyes beheld Father, Son and Spirit, the three who were one, Elohim. And though the fire burned bright above the throne, there was an overwhelming sadness that sank every heart in Heaven. Some angels clung to pillars while others hugged the ground and all were weeping. An audible sound of lament issued forth from the throne, terrible to all who heard.

Elohim's heart was once again broken and he wept the tears of a father for the loss of his children. He wept the tears of a god wounded by injustice and rebellion. He wept the tears of a creator to see the work of his hand and the object of all his love charge willfully and eagerly into destruction.

Gabriel threw himself before the throne and buried his face to the ground.

Clutching his robes he cried out, "Father! Why? Why? How can this be? Tell me this is not so. I have no strength left in me to see this foul thing upon the Earth. Father, why did we not use all our might to halt evil's progress while yet it was here in Heaven? Now is all lost and will grief be Heaven's portion forever? I cannot believe my eyes or my heart. This cannot be."

Gabriel pounded his fists on the ground.

"Father please, help me to see. For I have no hope that this will end in your happiness or any good. I have lost a friend and brother who is dead to me. And the beast of deception that rose in his place is now the destroyer of worlds. He has murdered love and torn Heaven's hope to pieces. Now beyond reach is the greatest joy of the Earth. It has slipped through our fingers and I fear none can save what is lost for all time. Elohim, Father, King of all creation, your broken heart condemns mine to eternal misery.

Tell me Father; what must be done? What can be done? Michael awaits and I am ready to do your bidding. Turn this tide for all things are within your grasp. Give me hope again. And win what you desire and let none stand in your way. End this thing Father. For your sake, end it now."

Gabriel was inconsolable. For after the rebellion of Heaven and all the grief he saw and knew, he could not imagine this could happen yet again, and certainly not with the children of Elohim. Though no angel or being in creation ever had such inner strength, fortitude, and confidence in Elohim as did Gabriel, here now this King of angels lay prostrate before his Lord as a beaten child cowering and weeping.

Elohim emerged from the fire and ever more in the appearance of an angel of light, he knelt beside Gabriel and lifted him to his breast.

"My faithful servant;" said Elohim, "you are truly my right hand and a joy to my heart. Weep now and let your heart be smitten but in the morning shall there be joy again. Your soft heart for me and for all of Heaven and my children below has reaped such sorrow. My heart is your heart and my pain is your pain. But take courage my son. Grief is for a season but love and joy is forever in my endless realm. All is not finished.

A blow and a dart have been delivered this day. Now is the time of evil upon the Earth. And the loss of life and love shall be bitter. But this terrible season will end. Hope, love and joy will rise as the sun in a blaze of light and warmth, that will cover the whole Earth and burn away all sorrow. This day will come; I promise you."

Gabriel raised his head to look into the sad eyes of his master as Elohim continued.

"I have kept my children from knowing all and seeing all for their own protection," spoke Elohim. "Today they have exchanged the truth of Elohim for a lie. They have not honored me and all thankfulness in their hearts has turned to selfishness. In their minds, they have said; 'who is Elohim?' And now the image they see is not the Father they have known. They have forgotten me and rejected me.

With their wills, they have said; 'we shall rule ourselves.' And Elohim no longer sits on the throne of their lives.

From their hearts they have said; 'who is Elohim that we should value him and desire and love him? Why should we worship and serve him? We shall value ourselves and love ourselves and worship and serve ourselves above all.'

But they have not yet known the whole of love and mercy and kindness and friendship with their maker. They know and see me only in part, and so have only rejected me in part. Their hearts have ventured into a distant and violent land of their own deception. Death has taken them today. And death they shall taste. They have lost their way and so they shall be lost from generation to generation.

But I tell you a mystery, Gabriel my son, that you might find strength yet this hour. There is still a way for them. Though my heart is broken, I shall not let go. A path of life and safe passage shall I place in this land of death. And for all who will, for every seeking, hungry heart that desires a way home, they will find the path that leads to life again. And I will sow seeds of truth in willing hearts. And one day many will look upon my heart and see my sorrow and know their folly and they will turn their hearts back to me. They shall have life and my love and I will have my children again. And every heart that turns again to the truth will indeed reap a harvest of love and friendship. And for those who choose death above life and love, they shall find an abode far from the one they have rejected."

Hope came to Gabriel. His heart became a little lighter.

"Father," said Gabriel; "what of those who will not and want not? Where shall they dwell? Is there not hope for all? Tell me Father is this path of life not for all?"

"Hope is for all my son. The path is for all. My desire is for all. But what of their desire? This have I told you before and still it is true, love is not love unless freely chosen. I cannot take the love they would withhold. It must be given to me. By compulsion, I cannot command friendship. For all power is mine and there is no thing in which I am restrained. For there is one King; one maker. There is none to rule the creator and master of all. But love is found in the choosing and giving. Love is won, not taken or plundered. All my power and love and strength shall I use to persuade and woo and win their hearts. But affection and devotion is theirs to give, not mine to take.

And if they say 'no' and 'never' to me then I shall honor that desire and twisted purpose and grant them safe passage far from my realm, to the furthest and most remote exile. In this place I am not. I do not rule there. I will not impose my will there. In this place a perverse freedom is granted - freedom from my love and rule. There, shall no thing of mine or my making reside. It is barren of all I am, prepared for those who desire none of me. This I will grant when all my devices fail.

But there is much to do before hope fades and hearts fail. And I am in need of a Captain and General to stand at my side. I am in need of courage and valor and strength and faith. Call Michael from his post. Stand together as brothers in arms. Martial your numbers. Be strong and prepared, for evil is upon the Earth. And you and Michael and all your host shall taste war. And the world of man will enter into darkness.

The battle begins. My Spirit will go before you. He will contend with wills and entice hearts in the world of man. But to you and Michael, his strength and your wisdom, I leave you the Adversary. You shall quarrel for your King. For I shall not lift my hand nor draw a sword until all is accomplished.

All our hopes hang by the thread of fragile hearts for which we will do battle.

But first, weep with me my son for a while. For I am wounded and all my compassions are kindled. And I shall go to see the children of my heart and see in their eyes the treachery and betrayal that wounds and pains me so."

Adam and Eve sat on the edge of the clearing staring at the tree from which they had eaten the fruit. The glow and warmth of light that had always emanated from them had vanished. There was until now always a cloak of gentle radiance illuminating their skin and softening their appearance. But now the cloak had been torn from them. As they looked at one another, they recoiled with discomfort at the new starkness and sharpness of their forms. They tried in vain to cover themselves as shame and self awareness stole their peace and confidence. They stood, as if naked before each other for the first time.

"What have we done?" said Adam. "Can we stand before Elohim? We have condemned ourselves to his chosen fate, for we are as ants to him."

Eve too bowed her head in hopeless sorrow for they knew that they had lost for themselves something grand and wonderful.

"We have eaten the fruit forbidden to us against his will and now will he smite us and cast us away with his great and awesome power."

"Why have we forgotten Elohim? Who are we to stand against such power?" cried Adam. "Oh that we could fasten this fruit back to this wretched tree. Oh that we could undo what has been done this day, for we are sure to suffer forever."

Elohim heard the fear and sorrow in the words of Adam and Eve. In angel form, he came into the garden and stood just a little way off within the thick belt of trees that lined the courtyard. It was the chosen and expected time of his daily arrival. But this day, he would not walk and talk with his children as on other days.

Elohim's heart was broken at the words he heard. For the words and thoughts of Adam and Eve were not of repentance but of regret. And though they would have turned back time to choose another course, it was not for love or honor or intimacy. It was for concern and fear of their woeful state and uncertain end. These were not the words of a child who longed for a father's forgiveness and comfort. This was the lament of one caught in the defilement of property not there own. Now facing judgment, they stood in their own minds as criminals, fearful in the face of a judge and ruler. For their false image of Elohim and the lies that lit the fires of rebellion had not diminished. Still, they envisioned a being not at all like Elohim. Though sorrow reigned that day in the garden, there was no advance toward trust and love and honor. They would rule their own hearts although justice was sure.

So sad this was to Elohim, for if true repentance was in their heart then all would have been restored that very hour. But they exchanged the truth of Elohim for a lie, and that could not be undone by sorrow or words. Still, Adam and Eve believed the harm was in the eating of the fruit that day. Never would they understand that it was not the tree but the betrayal of love and honor and the willing disregard of truth that broke Elohim's heart and brought death upon the land.

Adam and Eve both heard the sharp crackle of twigs under the feet of their maker as he strode into the clearing. Without word, they flew into the woods on the opposite side and hid behind a thicket. Their hearts were full of fear for surely, they thought, Elohim would strike them and wound them and cause great and terrible things to fall upon them. They knew his power but no longer remembered the love and compassion in his heart. Nor would they trust in mercy they had never known or needed. The words of the shadow continued to burn in their hearts and they imagined a vengeful, angry, powerful presence in the garden bent on their destruction.

There was little anger in the heart of Elohim but great sadness and pain at the loss of such a great treasure - the love and trust of his children. Still anger was there and would grow. Angry was he that these innocent children had bent their hearts toward their own destruction. And angry was he at the lies told that day and at the liar who, through deceit, won the hearts of his children. But the portion of pain and grief was the greater. And with unseen tears in his eyes, Elohim cried out to those who now feared him.

"Adam! Eve! Where are you?" he called. "Why are you hiding from me? What have you done this day? Why have you turned away from me and from love and reason? What have you believed in your heart that is now greater than that which you saw and heard and knew in me? Why have you done this thing and taken the fruit denied you for your own good? Come out of your hiding place and talk with me."

Adam and Eve slowly emerged from the trees and covering themselves as best they could shuffled slowly toward Elohim. They looked up to him but the light around him was too strong for their eyes and they looked away. He was terrible to look upon. They could not see his face through the light and his appearance was larger and bigger than ever they could remember. His voice was louder and more frightening. The closer they came the more fear they knew. And finally, falling on their knee before him, they raised their hands above their bowed heads as if expecting a blow.

But this day, Elohim was no different than the day before or the day before that. For the fall of his children did not alter the heart of their creator. He was the same as he ever had been and always would be. The eyes of Adam and Eve were opened to see what was not there. All their senses and sensitivities; their vision and awareness were corrupted and distorted. Their twisted hearts wrought twisted eyes. And that which their eyes saw confirmed that which their hearts imagined.

Elohim stood over his cowering children and longed to draw them close to him. He reached out his hands but to touch their heads. But Adam and Eve recoiled in fear.

Elohim withdrew his hands and said, "The path you have chosen is the path you will now walk until that path finds its end. This is your want and your choosing, not mine."

Elohim's voice rose to a roar as he called out into the trees before him, "Come forth and stand before me."

A shadow slipped in and out of viewing until it stood before the King of all creation.

A beast of beauty and colour whose skin was made of scales like jewels pranced into the clearing. As was its manner, it leapt high into the air from side to side to serpentine its way toward the gathering in the courtyard. Its graceful ballet came to a halt before Elohim.

Elohim asked the question again more stern than before; "Why did you do this thing?"

He looked to Adam, the stronger, larger and more aggressive of the two.

Adam shook with fear and said, "It is not my fault, my Lord, it is the woman. She tricked me into that which I was not willing."

Adam pointed his finger toward Eve.

Eve became angry at the accusation and scowled at Adam.

Adam suddenly felt indignant and mustered a new boldness. Standing upright he again said, "It's her doing, her fault, not mine. She deceived me."

He turned flustered and pointed his finger now at Elohim. "This woman... this woman!" said Adam, "whom you gave me, led me to this." Adam quickly realized his delicate position and hastily withdrew his finger, and once again, bowed his head unable to look directly at Elohim.

Eve raged at the accusation and quickly raised her finger in defense. She pointed it first at the beautiful dragon that stood before her and then to the shadow. It was not I for I too was deceived. It was this dragon, this... this... prancer, this serpent." She was uncertain who to blame but blame she would if it would free her from guilt and judgment.

"He told me... he forced me," she said. "It was his fault...their fault."

Eve hung her head and cried, now sure that there was no escaping some bitter end.

Satanas stood silent, fearful of Elohim but reveling in his victory this day. His heart was proud and brazen. Elohim turned to look at this fallen prince. Satanas turned away for he too could not look at Elohim. And there behind Elohim was Michael and Gabriel, though the fallen eyes of children could not see them.

A terrible silence hung over the clearing as Elohim seemed in no hurry to respond.

Finally the silence was broken and the voice of Elohim was low and thunderous.

"This day all of Heaven weeps for the loss of sight and knowledge," he said. "This day life gave way to death and truth gave way to lies. And the seeds you have sown shall reap a bitter harvest."

He turned to Adam "Oh that I could show you your error for it was not in eating or doing or disobedience. Far greater is the crime you have done this day. For you have wounded your King and friend to your own selfish end. Such is the betrayal and treachery of this day that all life will suffer. For Adam you are the first and Father of all mankind. And now you are the father of sin and selfishness, of suffering and of death. I made you to be Kings of the Earth and to rule as my children. But there is a new ruler in this land. His name is death and he shall rule with fear and loss and grief. And you shall bow to this new power for none shall escape his bitter reign.

Adam, do you see this garden of delights before you? It is but a small measure of all I have given you. The Earth and all creation was yours and under your command to serve you and aid you in all your ambitions. It was your friend and partner, this creation. It was an instrument and tool for you to built your dreams. And there was nothing that you could not accomplish with such a servant as the power of creation and the whole of Earth at your call and bidding.

But I cannot allow my creation to be a willing accomplice in your rebellion. That which served you will now serve its new master. For all of creation shall suffer and shall bow its head to death and chaos. Creation will resist you and hinder you and shall not hear your voice or obey your command. All that you seek to accomplish will be hindered by the chaos and disarray of the Earth and all its elements and parts. None shall stand with you. You shall subdue it now at great pain and cost.

The work of your hands will become a burden in this twisted creation. The sun shall burn your back and the wind shall chill your bones. Beast shall become your prey and you theirs. And the ground under your feet shall be harvested with strife and hardship. And all around you shall be a reminder of the bitter purchase you have made this day which is for you and all your children from generation to generation. Let this trouble bear the fruit of repentance and it shall lead you to a brighter tomorrow. This will be the choice for all generations until death reigns no more and all the Earth is bound together again in harmony and unity. That day of deliverance and promise, Adam you shall never see while you breathe."

Adam wept.

Elohim turned to Eve and pronounced judgment; but there was pain in his voice, "Eve my daughter, how fallen and distant you are. You may never know the pain that you have brought to your father. Children are for joy and now joy turns to grief. You too shall know the bitter sweetness of children. You shall know a greater pain in the birth of children. You and all your daughters shall give life to those you love with desire and delight fixed with the pain and tears. This shall be a reminder from generation to generation of the pain and love, the burden and the joy of children. You shall desire as do I, children for your heart but in their birth, you shall taste in small measure the pain of my heart."

Eve looked at Adam in anger and wondered if ever they would be together again. And if never, then little loss it seemed to her this hour, for they truly were broken apart and their oneness seemed only a distant dream.

Elohim looked to Eve and continued. "Eve," he said. "You shall indeed desire your husband and you shall birth in pain children for him. But this I see for you and all your generations that he will rule over you in power at the cost of love. For I have fashioned you from the same substance and equal in all respects. You were partners and allies and helpmates in all things for all generations. But I have also given you gifts different and diverse. For Adam is the stronger and equipped for provision and protection. His thoughts are not yours and yours are not his. Together you were blended to perfect that which the other was lacking. But now you will struggle and strive to build together. And your gifts shall compete with his for predominance. And man and woman shall push and pull at each other rather than pull and push together.

And in this struggle, the gifts and strengths given to man shall fulfill selfish ambition. The battle belongs to him. And rather than servant and friend, he shall be victor where there should never have been a contest. He will dominate and rule over you. This I see waiting for you down the path you have chosen. This is the walk of woman upon the Earth to never in life know that full and true harmony of man and woman until the day of reconciliation."

Eve Wept.

Elohim turned to the dragon of simple mind. And though only a beast, he willingly surrendered his shell to serve evil. And though he should not truly comprehend the judgment this day, Elohim would make an example of him for all generations.

"Serpent," said Elohim; "you and all your kind shall forever be a symbol of evil on the Earth, and your beauty is forfeit. For you are not unlike your possessor. He too was beautiful to look upon and a dragon in his heart. And now shall you crawl on your belly and eat dust all your days. And fearful you shall be for all who come across your path. The venom in you is the venom of Satanas - one to kill the body, the other to kill the soul."

And turning to Satanas in the oldest of language not understood by man or beast, Elohim spoke to the shadow.

"Look upon your victory today you father of lies," said Elohim. "You drew this woman into false confidence and led her down a path you know too well. She is your spoils and your spoiler. For I shall put enmity between you and her, between your seed and her seed. She is the mother of the Earth and all life comes through her womb. And though you have dealt her death today, she will birth your destruction. For in her is a seed and this seed is my seed planted to bear my fruit not yours. And this seed shall be passed from generation to generation until the day of my choosing. He shall place you under his foot and crush your head.

You dragon, you murderer of life and destroyer of dreams, you adversary of all; this I promise you as I am Elohim, Father of Creation and King of Heaven and Earth; though you shall bruise him on his heel and inflict your bitter venom, my son and seed shall be your end. He shall defeat death and take from you all that you have spoiled and plundered today. You have indeed already seen your end in that realm of utter darkness. And though you, in pride and arrogance, desire power and freedom, you shall have none. But you shall be flung into a prison of desolation. He shall usher you there, and never again shall you taste Earth's air or Heaven's light. Be warned, for this fragile victory you have won today will cost you everything tomorrow."

Satanas smiled.

15

The Dark Campaign

Adam and Eve knew nothing of what was said or was taking place but still cowered and waited for what they thought would be their end. They still had no hope in the goodness of Elohim and so no hope would be given.

Satanas bold as a lion, spoke to Elohim.

"Lord," petitioned Satanas, "may I be heard? For I have a matter of justice to which I desire satisfaction."

"Speak," answered Elohim.

Satanas mustered the sweetest voice he could conjure, as if Elohim could succumb to his deception.

"Are these not your children and heirs of Elohim?" asked Satanas. "Are they not fashioned in your image to reign with you and share in your eternal embrace? And are they not now the rulers of all the Earth? Still, they have seen fit to render their hearts agreeable to my position and contention. As you are the judge of all, is it not appropriate and equitable that their judgment stand in this place?

And surely their judgment should change the heart of Elohim who would unjustly banish Lucifer, the shining one. Am I not vindicated by the passing of their verdict?

And now by their own submission, should I not have rule of this realm? If power is theirs and they have sided with me then should I not stand as Lord of this place by their consent? And should you not continue to grant them all authority as is your word and promise and pledge? For the crown you have bestowed upon them is now freely given to me."

"Not so," said Elohim, "for though they have chosen to hear you and agree with you this day, they are still the heirs and rulers of this realm. Of this I shall not repent. But how shall they rule that which is defiant and ungovernable with hearts equally lawless and unrestrained? Where they in unity could master all, now in their rebellion, power shall be won in an endless struggle of flesh against flesh. They shall compete for power and the winner shall have it, but this is not my end for them. For now and for this season, all authority in the Earth is submitted to death and chaos and selfishness.

This too is your error. And though your ears are too deaf to hear and your eyes too blind to see, where I intended love to rule hearts and hearts to rule in love, now selfish ambition shall rule over the hearts of others.

But this I give you for it is true and you know it well; though you have no right to rule in this realm you shall indeed usurp the authority of imprisoned minds. Where they bend to your will, you shall have power in your grasp. But where they bend to mine, you shall have empty hands.

You cannot rule them against their wills and this realm is theirs to rule. But because of the misfortune of this day, you will purpose to rule through them so long as their hearts seek evil and malice. But the day shall come when no heart will abide you. Until that day, you are free by their authority to seek what you will and, with the consent of their twisted hearts, to do your foul deeds, and to rule and reign where their hearts bid you come.

But hear me. You shall not take their lives or bring death and destruction on them without cause or permission. They are the Lords of their own destinies and only those who have bent their knees and hearts to you shall you command or injure. Your power is no greater than theirs and they shall determine their path whether it be to repent and turn to me or to become tools in the hands of one such as you.

And this day, shall Michael and the legions of Heaven be your foe and stand against you to protect this realm and keep you from your every desire."

Satanas felt a sense of victory for surely he could rule these feeble minds. He clenched his fists and yelled out toward Heaven. "And what of mine and my host? Where are those who are for me but banished before ever they could stand with me? Do these children of Elohim not equally grant their petition in this place? If they stood beside me now, would not the Lords of the Earth have been agreeable to their cause? For they are not more than me but lesser in guilt, if guilt there is. Where is there justice for them?"

Elohim turned to Adam and Eve and speaking in the language of man said, "Your cruel imaginings, your unbelief and rebellion have unleashed an evil upon the Earth that only your devotion can harness. Beware, for a dragon and a lion wait at the door to pounce and kill. My heart is for you still and for a while I shall keep him at bay.

Go now from this place outside of this garden, for Elohim, Father, Son and Spirit have decreed that you shall not be as we are and shall not enter into the embrace of Elohim. So you shall not take from the fruit of the Tree of Life. It is denied you and you are barred from this place. For eternal life and bodies divine you have lost. And should you choose to seek this place or that tree, an angel shall slay you with a flaming sword before ever your foot touches this garden's earth."

An unnatural, cold wind blew through the garden and an eerie darkness ebbed over the evening sky. A horde of unseen angels flew from the mouth of a dark funnel not far from the garden. An army of the fallen were released into the Earth. Satanas bowed his head to Elohim, not in respect or honor, for he felt quite Elohim's equal at that moment. He flew into the air to gather his hosts. But not 100 meters in the air was met by Michael who stood in his path.

"Oh, Prince of angels," said Satanas, "have you come to wish and bid me well in this realm of mine?" Satanas laughed.

Michael's eyes burned bright.

"This is not your realm, my vulgar opponent," said Michael. "And what I wish you, I shall see done before this age is through. Elohim has spoken and I shall guard his will in this place. For all the ill-begotten power you take, you shall not exceed his limits. This space and air and earth is your domain. Your power shall not exceed the air of Earth. Neither Heaven nor any other creation shall be open to you. And know that your days are numbered in this place."

Satanas laughed and gloatingly said "It is enough, this Earth, this realm of man. I think I shall find a home here amongst Elohim's fools. It is enough."

As he began to fly away from Michael, he turned and looking back at the garden saw Elohim still standing over Adam and Eve. He turned again to Michael and said, "I think there is more to my will and power than you know, for today I have won my freedom and that of my host. So great a day; what shall I do tomorrow? More and greater than you can know. And my days shall I number myself. We shall meet again in battle and you shall not find me so docile in this place where I am the Prince of the power of the air."

Satanas flew with great speed to a far corner of the Earth as hordes of black shadows followed him.

Now, Satanas gathered his host together in a distant land and ruled them once again. He declared to them all that had taken place with the children of Elohim and in his twisted mind he looked the valiant hero and made Elohim the villain in the eyes of all. And having writhed in banishment in a dark and desolate place, they were ever more eager to serve their master. The malice of their Lord became their quest. For in their eyes he had saved them and would again before Elohim would cast them aside.

Now Gia came to his master's side and asked, "My Lord, have we won the day? For this taste of freedom is too great to surrender."

"We have!" said Satanas. "And we shall not surrender this freedom. We shall rule here in this place through the hearts of mankind. They shall do our bidding and we shall crush all flesh that will not."

"And what of Elohim and Michael and Gabriel?" asked Gia.

"Elohim has a plan and he is sure of it. But was he not very sure of his children and their loyalty? And in the strength of his hands was he not sure to keep them? And was he not sure as well of my impotence and disadvantage? Still I tore them from those strong hands where he failed to keep them. For this day, I have discovered that Elohim is less than I imagined. He now holds tight his plans in false confidence, but they can be torn from his failing fingers for I have done so. Yet while captive, I was able to win the greatest prize and spoil his dreams. And spoiler I shall be again."

"Do you know these plans, master?" asked Gia. Satanas answered "Elohim prophesizes that there shall come through this woman a man who is his son. This man shall cast me and all mine into darkness. He shall win the hearts of Elohim's children.

But do not worry, Gia, for Elohim has slipped. He has forewarned me too soon of his plot against me. He also told me that by my hand I would win a small victory. I shall wound this Son of Heaven. So says Elohim. And if wound be possible then murder shall be also."

"My master," asked Gia "I am in awe of your greatness, but I have seen too the power of Elohim. He can but blink an eye and we shall become dust. I fear his power of which we are not equal. And if he has the will to do this, how can it be thwarted?"

"I am not blind," said Satanas "we are no match for his power and we cannot defeat Elohim who has no beginning and no end. We shall win for ourselves eternal freedom from his rule and power. And we shall have this realm of Earth and sky."

Satanas moved closer to whisper as if Elohim could not hear every word from his throne in Heaven.

"Elohim has a great weakness," said Satanas. "And this weakness shall be a snare for him. He shall grant our demands."

"It seems that you my Lord have a plan as well," said Gia. "But what weakness does the creator of all have, for surely he lacks no thing?"

Satanas in pride divulged his plans and purposes.

"Elohim's weakness is that he loves and trusts and is just and fair," boasted Satanas. "He is bound by that which is in his heart and cannot deny himself. He lives by rules and principles that guide his actions. But we shall do and act by no such rules with no such boundaries. To my advantage, he loves too much. For he would do all and anything to save and protect and win back the hearts of his children. But they are close to being captive to my devices. Elohim cannot win what is mine and so we shall capture their wills to serve us and our ends.

Can you see Gia the light that left them just now in the garden. Their bodies fail and death is upon them. They will die and in their death they shall find no release from my grasp. They shall be mine. Elohim will see their complete ruin. And they shall stand with us in the day of judgment and their end shall be the same as ours, to be cast into darkness."

"And where is there victory in this?" asked Gia. "For the company of such for all eternity is no conquest at all."

"Elohim," said Satanas, "will not allow this. For I shall bargain with this King for the release of his children. His mercy and love will prevail and to win his children, he will need to satisfy my claim. I shall win for us all a pardon. For his just heart will pay any ransom to rescue what I have ensnared. He will pardon his condemned children and so shall we demand the same and more. His love is his undoing and his just and fair heart will bend to our purposes. He cannot exile the villain and not the children who serve the villain. His impartial compassion and love will insure an equal measure of mercy. And if his mercy fails then we shall see his misery and take his loved ones to the dark void. In time, he will relent and free all. Of this I am certain."

"And what of Michael and Gabriel and the promised one, the son of our destruction?" asked Gia.

"Elohim has withdrawn his hand from the battle. Michael is now our great enemy in this place. But he too has a weakness. For he loves the children of Elohim and they shall be a shield for us. He will be slow to act and quake at the prospect of their destruction. And then we will rally our strength and take him down. Elohim will seek to free him as well from our grasp."

Satanas hesitated and then spoke again in a close whisper. "As for the man of Elohim's promise. He is not yet a man. He is seed sown in the woman that will pass from generation to generation. And if even the man we could not hinder, the seed we can surely destroy. And to halt this prophesy and promise is to assure our rule here on Earth."

"How shall we destroy the seed?" questioned Gia.

"Destroy the people and the seed will die," said Satanas.

"But are we not forbidden to take lives not surrendered to us?" asked Gia.

"We need not raise our hand to kill," answered Satanas; "for we shall forge greater weapons to do our bidding. The children of Elohim shall be both our allies and our foe. They shall be both our employed assassins and our unsuspecting prey. For I see in their hearts a shift. I can see that their minds grow feeble and their bodies will weaken from generation to generation. And with little enticement, they shall amend their purposes and forget that they are the children of the most high. Their reckless fall shall be our strength. We shall raise up armies of men to destroy at our command. We shall breed hatred and malice in the hearts of men and they shall do warfare against their own. The seed shall die at the hands of the very ones he comes to protect."

Gabriel and Michael stood before Elohim. The whole of Heaven was in tears and Elohim sat on his throne. With a voice of compassion he spoke to his hosts.

"All is not lost my children for times and epochs will bring an end to this sorrow and joy will come in like a flood. And what pain and grief there is I shall bear it for the sake of my children. Here is hope today for all. I will birth a son who was and is and will always be. He is our hope and our future. He will bear upon his back the weight of all grief and all pain. He shall set captives free and restore all things. He shall end terror and banish anarchy. He will destroy the destroyer. His name is wonderful. His name is peace. His name is healing. His name is redemption. He is the one who will set my people free. Let all the Earth and all Heaven know that I AM."

And that day, and every day since, hope burned bright in Heaven as bright as Elohim who sits upon his throne in the heart of Heaven. And Elohim sent forth his Spirit into all the Earth for all generations that they might see him and know him. And Gabriel and Michael and their host still keep watch over the children of Elohim.

Epilogue

Chapter One

So began the great and terrible War of the Seed. Satanas drew out all his strength and ordered his legions to fix themselves to the affairs of man above all else. And from generation to generation, the powers of great darkness sought both the allegiance and the annihilation of the children of Elohim and the seed of promise. Most of all they sought to bring grief and harm to Elohim.

Now Adam and Eve, being turned out of the garden, found a home in a hard but fertile land. The curse upon the Earth would not yet reach its peak for generations. Still life was hard and they ever pined and longed for the garden and life they lost. The turning of their hearts brought doubt, fear and suffering as trust was shattered and hope grew thinner. With every passing day, their bodies grew weaker and the power of their minds diminished. They turned their hearts back to Elohim but failed to ever find freedom from the lies and deceptions that clouded their reason and reaped a harvest of death. And though they walked in tempered obedience and fragile loyalty, all was not as it should be. For fear of Elohim more than love now ruled their hearts. And through the centuries of lives and the generations of their children, innocence decayed and devotion ebbed and flowed from season to season.

As with all generations to follow, a challenge to Elohim's rule seethed and lingered in every being. And the words of the serpent infected sensibilities and laid siege to the wills of man. For their passions were predisposed to seek their own good and happiness above that of Elohim's and their fellow man. Still, with Elohim's aid and strength, Adam and Eve and many who followed subdued the powers within that would tear them from all hope and Elohim's hands.

Some followed Elohim and bent their wills to his will. Many others became fodder for powers of malice on the Earth.

The tales and stories of the War of the Seed are best told in chronicles other than these.

Though powers gathered and schemed and laid in wait, the battle began in earnest with a strike and a blow. Cain slew Abel and drew the first blood of the children of Elohim by hands meant for greater, purer things. Satanas and his Generals were not far off when sacred blood touched the soil of the Earth for the first time. Human ears could not hear that day the revelry of such a victory. But all of Heaven heard and winced in grief and burned in fury that such could happen not far from the garden in which love and friendship once dwelt.

In the generations that followed, the black powers grew strong upon the Earth. Satanas became a student of creation and learned its secrets. And with the same zeal with which he once painted Heaven's halls and filled its air with symphonies of his own design, he now perfected his black arts to turn the beauty of Elohim's gift against his children.

And Satanas ruled forces of malice to inflict the inhabitants of Earth. And in his quiver were darts and arrows of plague and pestilence, of pain and torment, blight and pest.

And of all the weapons he fashioned, the greatest still were the lies and deceptions that turned Kings into slaves and warriors into servants. He used all his devices to hinder mankind from truth and light. And fearful was Satanas that any should see the truth and find the way. And all his deceptions were designed to keep man from seeing and knowing and understanding. Illusions and fantasies were forged in the hearts of man. Veils of darkness were pulled over their eyes to keep them from sight. Hearts were darkened to keep them from light.

And two great fears did Satanas have that any should see with true eyes and enlightened hearts Elohim, the great King, and to know his love and character and purposes. And of equal peril to his charade was that they might discover, either by their own devices or by the Spirit of Elohim, their own royal lineage that they are the children of Elohim and heirs of the Kingdom of Heaven.

Now the history of man is full of tragedy and triumph, of peril and pleasure and of war and peace.

And as the violence ebbed and flowed in the world of man, the war in the unseen realm continued unabated. Whether a war of words or power, it was in all realms a war of life and death, of good and evil, of light and darkness and all was a battle between the truth of Elohim and the bitter lies of the fallen Archangel Lucifer. And the prize was always the children of Elohim who were both villains and victims in this struggle of flesh and spirit.

About the Author

Bill Payne, born and educated in Canada, now lives in Spain with his family. An ordained minister, he has been in full time Christian ministry and education for 25 years. He continues to work with and represent Youth With A Mission; an international Christian Mission Organization with operating locations world wide.

His experience includes Church planting, the development of new ministries, oversight of major international projects such as the 1988 Olympic Outreach in Seoul, Korea; the 1992 Olympic Outreach in Barcelona, Spain. He has also initiated multiple training programs for Christian discipleship, missions and ministry.

Bill served as Dean for the College of Christian Ministries in the University of the Nations in Hawaii and continues to serve on the international board as an Assistant Dean.

He has lectured in over forty countries and lived on three continents. An in demand speaker, he continues to travel and speak in schools, churches, seminars and conferences worldwide. He has written several books and contributed to ministry and mission resources in use around the globe.

His email address is: billpayne2@hotmail.com

Printed in the United States
107455LV00001B/4-102/A